# THE FLORIDA MOTEL

JAY GILBERT

# THE FLORIDA MOTEL

By Jay Gilbert



Cover by Paradox Book Covers

Worldwide Electronic & Digital Rights

Worldwide English Language Print Rights

ISBN - 978-1-950940-13-4

Published by SeaQuill Press, LLC Jupiter, Florida, USA

Created with Vellum

# 1

# HELGI

R*ing-ring...Ring-ring...Ring-ring*

"Front desk, can I help you?"

"Number nine number nine number nine—"

"Hello...can I help you?"

"Number nine number nine number nine—" A deep hum emanated through the switchboard headset.

*Huh?* "Uh...hello? Are you ok, sir? Do you need help?" I asked.

"Number nine number nine number nine—"

*What the hell?* "I'm hanging up now."

"Number nine number nine number nine…"

"Hey, somebody...anybody...get out here right now!" I shouted over my shoulder.

"I'm coming, I'm coming, hold your horses," Mom said from the living quarters behind the front desk.

Passing through the door into the office, Leena Moe made a grand entrance. Her head adorned with huge curlers, attempting to do something—exactly what I'm not sure—with that thin, Finn hair of hers. Ma was 5'4, a hundred forty pounds with Nordic pale skin and a smile attached to the biggest heart in the world that brightened the room when she entered.

"Ma, there is something really strange going on in room nine"

"What's up Helgi?" she asked.

"I don't know, but the guest in number nine keeps calling the switchboard and chanting 'number nine number nine number nine' over and over. I tried asking if he needed help, but—"

*Ring- ring...Ring-ring...Ring-ring…*

"There he is again. You take it this time."

Just then, a station wagon turned into the motel and up to the office. I could see the faces of the parents as they pulled up to the office. They looked dead tired after a long day on the road with a car full of rambunctious kids. The dad had clearly surrendered to screams from the back seat. "*Please*, Daddy, stop at the one with the pool." Peering out the front of the all glass office, I greeted them with a smile. Station Wagon Dad got out of the car and walked through the front door of the office.

"You help the guest. I'll answer the phone," Mom instructed.

"Good afternoon, sir. Welcome to the Florida Motel."

"We need a room for the night," the dad said with a look of defeat on his face.

"How many will be staying in the room?"

"Two adults and two kids."

"We have a nice room out by the pool with two double beds. Will that work?"

"Sounds good."

"Great. Please fill out the registration card," I said, handing him the card and a pen.

Meanwhile, Mom grabbed the large metal jack attached to a thick red cord leading to the underbelly of the antique WWII-era switchboard. She plugged it into the hole labeled "nine" while simultaneously placing the headset over her ear. Working the switchboard was like that scene from *Twenty Thousand Leagues Under the Sea* when Kirk Douglas fought the giant squid. While there were electronic telephone systems in 77', why would Dad have replaced a perfectly good switchboard? I'll tell you why ...he was cheap, cheap, chcap!

"Hello, may I help—"

"Number nine number nine number nine," the voice echoed in the headset.

"Sir, can I—"

"Number nine number nine number nine...." Mom kept trying to break in, but no luck. The chanting continued.

"I'll hang up and see what happens," she said.

A good plan, until she pulled the plug out of the switchboard. The ringer automatically sounded off to alert the operator of an incoming call.

Since most small motor lodges were run by couples with maybe a hired maid or two, they needed to multi-task. As a result, oftentimes someone wasn't physically in the office waiting for a car to pull up or the switchboard to ring. Fortunately, these old switchboards were designed to get your attention. They only had one volume level. Loud—spine-shattering, ear-piercing—L.O.U.D!

Station Wagon Dad finished the registration and glanced at the switchboard as he handed me a credit card, his brow raised in question. I put the card in the mechanical imprinter, placed the multi-carbon-copy form on top, and pushed the metal handle back and forth. *Thwonk, thwonk* and the credit card information was embossed onto the form. I really needed to get him out of the office before "number nine" scared him away and down the road to the Bambi Motel.

*Ring-ring...Ring-ring* screamed forth as Mom pulled the plug then immediately put it back in.

"Front desk, can I help you?" she answered, all sweetness, as if it were the first time he called.

*Oh, for the love of God.* My eyes rolled to the back of my skull.

I froze when I heard her say, "Sir...ah...umm...we'll be right over."

"Be right over?" I protested with both confusion and fear. I knew "we'll be right over" meant *I* would be right over. There was no *we* about it.

"It was the only thing I could think of to get him to stop alright?" she shot back.

"Here are your keys, sir, and some extra towels for the kids to use at the pool." Station Wagon Dad's expression had turned from curiosity to concern. I needed to distract him and do something extra to make him feel good and leave the office.

"The ice machine is outside next to the office. Take as much as you need. Thank you for choosing the Florida Motel." I said while gesturing him to the door.

"Helgi, go over to number nine and knock on the door," Mom said in an empathetic, yet, you-have-no-choice-I'm-going-to-win-the-battle-so-you-might-as-well-go-without-protest-and-get-it-over-with manner. Then she started to review the daily room log for tomorrow's check-outs, stay overs and reservations like any other routine day. Clearly a tactic to change the conversation.

"Anyone else around?" I inquired. "Dad, Gainesville PD, the National Guard?"

"Nope, you're it."

"You don't say."

"No, you don't say, I do," she scolded.

"Great, I'm the only one around, so I get to knock on the door of a psychopath!"

"Don't whine, consider it a compliment. Heck, it's a promotion."

"Do I get a raise?"

"No, you get food and a roof over your head."

"I love you too." I said. "Ma...please...let's call the police."

"We only call the cops when we absolutely need them, like for robbers, pimps and prostitutes. We don't want to be the motel that cried wolf. Now go over there and see if anything strange is going on."

"Geesh. Ya think something strange may be going on? Whatever gave you that idea?"

My protest was minor league compared to that stubborn Finn mother of mine. I had already lost the battle before she finished her request...err...directive.

Reluctantly, I left the safety of the office and made my way out to Room Nine. The oppressive Gainesville heat permeated every inch of my body. Laden with humidity, the air painted me in perspiration. Like whitewashing a fence, hot liquid slopped over my skin and under my clothes. Approaching the room, I pictured my blood mixed with sweat, pooling on the sidewalk as the cops outlined my body with chalk. My heart pounded in my chest as the chanting became audible.

"Number nine...number nine...number nine…"

I knocked on the room door. "Maid service," squeaked from my cotton-dry throat. "Do you need anything… extra towels, soap?" *Maybe a new needle for your pock marked arms you friggin' junkie.* No answer, nothing, zippo, nada.

I desperately wanted to get out of there but knew I had to give it one more try before returning to the office and reporting to Sergeant Major Mom.

I waited, knocked again and then loudly announced, "MAID SERVICE!"

Between the summer heat and fear for my life, face-dripping, shirt-drenching sweat poured from every part of my body. I was soaking wet.

The chanting abruptly stopped. The doorknob turned and the old, sun-faded wooden door opened as far as the attached security chain allowed. A cloud of marijuana smoke rolled out of the room like fog. Foggy also described the guest peering out at me through the crack. Scraggly shoulder-length hair, crooked yellow teeth, shirtless with cutoff jeans. he...it...leaned into the doorjamb using his forehead as a brace to stand upright.

"Yeah? What the fuck you want?" the stoner asked as if offended by my presence.

Sa-sa-sorry to bother you sir, but your phone rang at the front desk. Is everything ok?"

What phone? You didn't call my room."

Ah, no, sir, I didn't say we called you. You called us."

"Who called me?"

"No, we called me...I mean you- you called.

"You called you? Why would you do that?" he said.

*What the fuck? This guy's wasted and smelly.*

"I don't need any pizza," he said.

*Ookeedookee, buddy. This dude's totally fucked up.*

But, as Fogman turned away to close the door, something flashed in my eyes. The midday sun streaming through the cracked door reflected off the huge knife he held behind his back. He was too many doobies into his day to figure out that your back faces the door when you turn around.

"Ah...umm...sorry to bother you."

As I cautiously backed away from the door, the chanting resumed. "Number nine...number nine...number nine..."

Crap, I was only joking about that whole outline of my body thing!

"Shit! Shit! Shit!" I yelled, bursting through the office door.

"What's the matter; what happened now?" Mom inquired nonchalantly.

"What happened? What happened!? What the hell do you think happened? Oh, I know, you thought he needed some new soap, clean towels or nine pizzas delivered to his room! He's a fucking nut case strung out on drugs, chanting number nine and oh yeah...HE'S GOT A BFK!"

"BFK?" she asked.

"Big Fucking Knife!" I shouted.

"Watch your mouth." Mom warned.

"Watch my mouth? Are you fucking kidding me?"

"There you go again," she said, expressing her disapproval of my language instead of showing some inkling of parental concern for her offspring.

"Call the cops right now or I will."

"Settle down, Helgi," she cautioned. "If we called the police every time a guest appeared a bit strange, we'd get a bad reputation and people wouldn't come here to stay. That money pays for your tuition and books."

*Great, let's add extortion to indentured servitude.*

"I will have Sven go have a talk with him when he gets back from picking up chemicals for the pool boy."

"You mean me."

"Yup," she said matter-of-factly.

Better that than paint for the painter. You guessed it. That would be me as well. I hated painting in the summer. Pool boy duty was much better as I could always jump in to cool off.

"In the meantime, Helgi, I'll watch the switchboard. You need to get the laundry going," she directed. "We need clean sheets and towels for the lunch business."

# 2

# HELGI

My name is Helgi. In the late seventies, I helped my parents, Sven and Leena Moe, run our motel while I attended the University of Florida. Back then, I dreamed of one day having a normal job, with a normal company, and most of all a normal life. Now, there's nothing normal about running a motel. It's more akin to a state of insanity. But a family business requires…well… family, which is a form of indentured servitude, a commitment of sorts. I was a prisoner, committed to life in an insane asylum. And like any good prisoner, I thought about escaping. Every. Day.

The Florida Motel was the type of lodging where you parked right in front of your room. A narrow sidewalk hugged the building, and a rust-colored awning, that looked like it held on to the roof for dear life, protected you from the elements. Built in the thirties, it looked much the same as any other roadside motor lodge. The only difference was the basic layout. Most were a one-story row of rooms configured in the oh-so-original shapes of the letters I, L or, in our case, the uber-luxurious U. Gotta love alphabet architecture. Some also had a swimming pool. Usually next to the parking lot, a pool was another form of marketing. We also had a big flamingo-pink slide and a diving board.

Our little old motel was on the road in southwest Gainesville. You know, "the road," otherwise known as US 441. The one that connects such historic and colorful places like Weeki Wachee Springs, where you could see "real" mermaids, Indian River fruit stands and souvenir shops with names like Shells, Seashells, or, my favorite, Shell World.

Families traveling north on the road had to cross Paynes Prairie. A swampy wetland filled with alligators, water moccasins, ducks, egrets and herons. If it crawled, flew, swam or slithered, it lived in the prairie. Great blue heron would fly along the road like B52 bombers escorting weary travelers out of danger and to their destination. In the distance, an amazing sight would appear before their eyes. An enormous, blue State of Florida, wrapped in neon lighting with a wedge-shaped marquee fitted into the panhandle, towered over the road. Every motel lodge had its own unique neon sign, beckoning travelers to turn in and stay awhile. Our sign was spectacular—even iconic to Gainesville. At the bottom were white neon letters with the words VACANCY and NO that could be turned on or off separately. Even if we had rooms available, we still lit up the NO around midnight. Hey, we couldn't keep Grandma up all night manning the front desk. She had to take her teeth out sometime.

# 3

# HELGI

*Nooners. I have to do laundry for the damn Nooners. Christ, I can't wait for classes to start. At least that will get me the hell out of here for a few hours of sanity.*

The lunch business was better known as "Nooners." These weren't tired people needing a cat nap or happily married couples getting away from the kids for some alone time. Nooners were cheaters. Cheating was so common in the biz it provided a constant and reliable source of income to the motel. We should've had a separate line item in the books like Nooners, Cheaters or how about Other Misc. *Inncum.*

It was my job to clean the first two to three open rooms from early morning checkouts. They needed to be ready for the noon business. This usually meant the smaller, single rooms, if empty. They were quicker to clean than the larger doubles. It also kept the love birds contained to one bed, which would have to be cleaned again before travelers checked in for the evening. Nooners liked the anonymity of being away from the activity of the office and the rooms next to the entrance made for a quick getaway once the deed was done. Hopefully, we had some rooms out at the ends.

Nooner rooms were cleaned like any other check-out…sort of. The requirements upon their departure were…shall we say…a little loose? I mean, really, we knew what they were doing, where and for how long, usually about thirty minutes…or less. They seldom pulled down the bedspread and never used the linens—other than the washcloths. Their attention was elsewhere, and time was of the essence.

All I needed to do was straighten the bed, clean the toilet, give the shag a quick vacuum, and replace the washcloths. The most observant customer couldn't tell the difference, especially after a long day on the road.

"Seven, ten, and sixteen are ready," I reported. "We're out of towels, and Hester's not here yet to start the laundry. I've got to go to class."

"Oh no, room sixteen doesn't have clean towels?" Mom said in a panic. A couple had already checked in.

*It's only 11:30am! Getting off to an early start today.*

"So?" I inquired, as if I didn't know what she meant.

"Here, take these over to them right away," she said handing me a set of clean towels.

We always had a few towels, soaps, and toilet paper stashed in the front desk in case of an emergency, or if it was late at night, the lucky one on duty didn't have to unlock the door and go to the laundry room for supplies.

Our security system involved locking the office door at sundown and serving guests through a small, movie theater-like window. You know; the ones where you can barely slide money under the slot. After payment, we slide the room keys out to our guests.

"Ma, they don't want clean towels. Hell, they don't want *any* towels," I said in a cynical voice.

"Take the towels."

"But…"

"No buts, take them over now!"

It wasn't the "but" I worried about. It was the "butts." Oh well, yet another futile exercise on my part to convince Leena of anything once she made up her mind.

The noon guests hadn't been in room sixteen, a small single out next to the road, more than five minutes when I arrived at the door. I timidly knocked on the door hoping to sneak away without being noticed and yet report to Mom that I tried, but no one answered.

No answer.

*Ok, one more time.* Horrified at the prospect of interrupting a quickie in progress still wasn't as bad as facing my mother back in the office with undelivered towels in hand.

I knocked again, this time louder and with fear-driven urgency.

"Yeaaa," a deep, make that a Barry White-deep voice reverberated from within.

"Ta-ta-Towels, sir, clean towels," I responded in my best, please-don't-kill-me voice, followed by an audible "Gulp."

Nothing but dead silence followed for what felt like an eternity.

*I'm going to slowly step away. I'll tell Mom they didn't want the damn towels and sent me packing.*

As I began a slinky, crouch-and-turn maneuver, the

doorknob turned. I froze. The door cracked open enough for a huge black hand to emerge. It reminded me of Thing on the TV show *The Addams Family*. Remember Thing, the creepy hand in a box?

"Sa-sa-sorry for the inconvenience sir," I blurted, trying to say anything that remotely made sense at that moment. The motel biz had a knack for putting me in uncomfortable situations requiring a "Sa-sa-sorry."

I placed the towels in Thing's hand, which immediately grabbed them and quickly disappeared back inside. The door abruptly shut. Mission accomplished, I stopped by the laundry room to make sure enough towels were ready and *in* the rooms before the next set of Nooners arrived.

About thirty minutes later the "guests" checked out. Since Nooners always prepaid in cash, they left the keys on the nightstand, hopped in their cars and rolled on down the road. This was the first form of Express Checkout.

# 4

# HELGI

Entering the laundry room in August was like stepping into a poor man's sauna. Imagine for a moment, hundred-degree temps with nearly the same humidity. It was a hole-of-a-room with no AC and only a small jalousie window in the back to give one the impression of ventilation.

Like all good, fleabag motels, we *had* to wash the sheets and towels when guests checked out. With nineteen rooms and customers coming and going daily, we *needed* to unstick, de-stain, and otherwise delouse the linens. For health department reasons, we were required to use hot water in the commercial-grade washer. The dryer finished the job with blast-furnace temps, torching the sheets and towels to a perfect, board-stiff dry. The two appliances radiated an intolerable amount of heat and moisture into the stifling little hotbox.

Drenching wet didn't come close to describing the air in that room. Maybe the Amazon rainforest, on the equator, high noon, right after a torrential downpour paints a better picture? I felt drier holding my breath under water while brushing stains on the bottom of the pool.

As each load finished, it had to be folded and stacked in that damn little hotbox torture chamber called the laundry room.

I had to get out of there. Getting a college degree was my ticket to normalcy. In the meantime, I somehow needed to survive this Shakespearean comedy.

# 5

# HELGI

Hester, a tall, rail-thin black woman, with dark, smooth skin, and a large afro, was our full-time maid. She was super nice and evoked a warm, welcoming feeling that said, "Come here child, you needs a hug." Her babies, as she called them, may have been born in the hood, but they couldn't have had a better, more loving mama. Hester was a down-to-earth, hard-working, decent human being.

She was also a working machine. We paid her hourly, but you would have thought we paid her by the room. She had a method of cleaning rooms efficiently and effectively. She knew all the tricks of the trade and taught me everything I needed to know…about cleaning rooms.

"Hester, how do you clean these rooms so fast? It takes me twice as long as you," I asked.

"Come here, baby. I shows you how it's done," she replied. "First, you load up the cart proper. You don't want to make a bunch of trips to the laundry room to refills it."

The cart stood two feet wide, four feet long and waist high to me. Open on one of the long sides and closed on the other, it had built in shelves to carry sheets and towels.

The top, basically a huge tray, held a stockpile of toilet paper, tissue boxes, and those little motel soaps and shampoo bottles. On the front end was a canvas laundry bag for dirty sheets and towels, at the other end a large, plastic garbage bag. Both bags hung through metal hoops, which held them open, making it easy to simply dump linens or trash while cleaning rooms. On the driver's end of this monstrosity was a small shelf at the bottom with a bucket filled with cleaners, toilet brush, etc. and room for a vacuum. Did I say "small" shelf?

Made of heavy gauge metal, with sharp corners, this thing was a mini tank on wheels. Best give it a wide berth for fear of gashing your leg wide open and bleeding to death. Unfortunately, both the inventory of clean linens and the capacity of both the garbage and laundry bags were good for only five or six rooms. Unless you were Hester, who could have been an engineer by the systematic way she loaded the cart.

"I's only makes one or two trips to reloads," she said. "Ms. Leena will let you know if a room is a checkout or stay-over."

We came to the first room of the day; Hester knocked on the door and announced, "Maid service."

She glanced over her shoulder at me. "Even if I knows it be a checkout, I always knocks and tellsm I'm here. You never knows what you might be seeing when you opens the door." Hester paused for a few seconds to see if someone responded. Convinced it was empty, she shoved the key into the knob, flung open the door and grabbed a bucket filled with cleaners and the toilet brush all in one seamless motion. "Now look here, baby. You begins in the bathroom and works your way out. Start with the yucky. Finish with the tucky."

Hester began cleaning so fast I could hardly keep up while trying to make mental notes. Comet Cleanser erupted like a volcano at the working end of her pencil-thin arm. Covering the tub, sink and toilet without dropping a single fleck of the green, flourlike stuff on the floor, she scrubbed, rinsed and then flushed the mushy remains of the little soaps.

By the way, whoever the hell ever came up with the idea to mold an indented soap holder into a sink that doesn't drain should be shot or at least forced to be a maid for a week.

"Hopefully we don't run into a clogged drain or toilet. It be our job to fix it before callin' for Mr. Sven," she said.

"Nice," I replied in a snarky tone.

"On the weekends you be Mr. Fixit, honey," Hester said with a grin.

Usually the cleanup was a simple matter of grabbing hair out of the drains or a good plunge in the bowl to get things moving again. You'd be amazed, if not gagged, by what we discovered in the plumbing. Why do people behave like animals when they stay in motels? Anyway, back to Room Cleaning 101 with Professor Hester.

"Once you be done with the bathroom, take a used towel and wipes the tub and sink so's they looks dry and shiny. Otherwise, Ms. Leena be gettin' a call at the front desk demanding another room as 'This room has not been cleaned. The tub and sink are still wet!'" she said, mimicking a pompous guest.

Hester continued her lecture as she moved through the room. "Don't be lookin' inside the trashcan. You might see somethin' that'll bring up your breakfast. Just grabs a corner, pulls it across the top, close, lift n' takes it to the cart. Drop n' turn back into the room. You always be moving, baby. Never stops to rest," instructed Professor H as she emptied the ash trays into the waste baskets.

"Aww come on. No union breaks?" I whined. She shook her head, pulled out the feather duster and started dusting and the nightstands, dressers and windowsills.

"Clean the windows only if there be something on the glass. Elsewise, leave em for when they gets foggy from cigarette smoke."

Stripping the bed, she inspected the bedspread.

"Look for any food stains or other stuff. We haves to wash n' dry it if it be soiled. Iffen it be clean, lays it over a chair and strip the sheets and pillowcases. Again, don't look; start in one corner, lift, pull, gather the sheets into one large bundle and dumpem' in the laundry bag." Hester taught with the same efficiency and directness as her work.

"Whoa, don't look?" I asked. "What if I put my hand in something gooey?"

"You don't want to see it, and nuthin' ever gets on the sides anyway," she said.

Hester's bed-making was an art form. I watched in amazement. Starting with the bottom sheet, she tucked it in-between the mattress and box spring on all four corners. Then, while standing near the headboard, grasping the corners of both the top sheet and bedspread in one hand she extended her other arm, grabbed the middle and with one, upward sweeping motion, flew everything over the bed. Filling with air, the linens literally sailed across the bed and landed perfectly flat on the mattress. A bit of tucking and the bed was made. Like a ballroom dance, Hester effortlessly flowed around the room, each step orchestrated by an inner, soulful melody.

"Make sure the bedspread completely covers the pillows with a little tuck under em. This gives the bed that clean, tidy motel look, she said. "It be the first thing peoples see when they comes in the room. Iffen' the bed be clean and neat with the pillows all tucked in; they be happy. When the guests be happy, Ms. Leena be happy, and I haves a job."

"Well, we need to keep Ms. Leena happy now don't we," I said grinning.

"Ok, baby, gets the vacuum, plug it in near the door and go to the far corner of the room."

The vacuum, also industrial grade, sounded like a jet engine attached to wheels and a bag. This thing put a freshly mowed...err...vacuumed look on the two-inch-thick deep green shag carpet and left no dirt behind.

"Works your way backwards out of the room so's you don't leave any footmarks on the carpet," she advised.

The very last step was to shoot a blast of commercial grade air freshener into the room and quickly shut the door before that shit hit your lungs.

Now, that lesson was for check-outs. We also had stay-overs and Nooners. You might expect a Nooner room to be the grossest to clean, but, they were the easiest and least gross.

Stay-overs were customers who spent more than one night at the motel. This was common on football weekends when fans were in town to see the mighty Gators play at Florida Field. In fact, almost every motel, including ours, had minimum two-night stays for football weekends. This was simple supply and demand. We even doubled the rates for the home games.

There were also the families of people getting treatment for something bad at Shands Teaching hospital at UF. You didn't go to Shands for a cold, flu or appendectomy. People were there for days or even weeks and their families had to stay somewhere.

In any event, stay-overs were like Nooners, with a bit more cleaning, but nothing like a checkout.

It was vexing that I knew this much detail about cleaning motel rooms but couldn't keep macro vs. microeconomics straight in my head. Maybe if college professors taught like Professor Hester, we would have learned something useful.

# 6

# HELGI

"Nooner rooms are clean; laundry's started, and Hester is here," I shouted to Mom. "I've got to get going or I'll be late for class."

"Ok, don't go to the library to study as we need you on the front desk after dinner tonight."

*Thanks for the words of encouragement. How am I supposed to pass my classes if I don't have time to study?* "Will do, see ya later," I yelled, sprinting out the door before she could assign another task.

Campus was less than two miles away straight up 13th Street, which is also US441 or "the road", but it might as well have been two thousand miles at this rate.

I drove a 1976 Plymouth Volare Road Runner. I know a 76' wasn't a "real" Road Runner. Instead, it was an anemic-federal-smog-emissions-screwed-up stepchild of its 60s' namesake. Couldn't even burn rubber. But it was painted baby blue, had stripes along the sides, a horn that went "meep meep," and most of all, it was my first car...'nuff said.

Dad helped me with the purchase by cosigning the loan. “Don’t screw up my good credit. Make the payments on time…with your own money,” he commanded.

I had to make the payments, but Dad, being from Minnesota, decided I didn't need to spend extra for A/C…not even in Florida. So, driving it in the summer was like driving the laundry room down the road.

Pulling onto 13$^{th}$ Street, I headed up to campus and passed under the viaduct. I glanced over to see if anything new had been added to the retaining wall where local artists—mostly drunk students—painted murals depicting the campus life. Sometimes scenes from the *Kama Sutra* appeared in graphic detail. The resulting rubbernecking by drivers caused numerous rear-enders. Unfortunately, city or campus maintenance workers would immediately paint over them.

I always cut through campus on Museum Road on my way to the dreaded commuter lot, taking care to drive 19 mph to ensure I didn’t break the 20-mph speed limit. Exceed it by one mile per hour and you’d get pulled over by one of the campus catch n’ fine police. Dropouts from the highway patrol or Gainesville P.D, they all resembled cloned Barney Fifes.

Slowly making my way through campus, I faced the greatest challenge of all. DWC (Driving with Coeds.) UF had the hottest, most beautiful women of any college bar none. They all wore tiny, form-fitting halter tops and butt-cheek-exposing short shorts as they walked to and from their classes. It was like driving through a life-sized, three-dimensional issue of *Playboy*. On every corner a centerfold appeared before my eyes. They walked, jogged and rode bikes. Oh God! The bike riders! Imagine a Playboy bunny, wearing Daisy Dukes, a tiny, skin-tight top that barely holds her huge, firm titties, riding bent over the handlebars of a ten-speed bike. I'm not sure which I enjoyed more, watching them coming or going. I was an eighteen-year-old, testosterone-raging virgin. I couldn't stop thinking about getting laid…all the time.

Things only got worse when these coeds, sweating from the hot summer sun, walked into the freezing cold classrooms. I think the dirty old professors kept it that way on purpose. Upon hitting the ice-cold air in the classroom, all the girls' "girls" came to attention. How the hell did they expect us to pay attention to the lecture during a parade of erect nipples?

After making it through the DWC gauntlet, it was time to hunt for a parking spot. The commuter lot existed for all us sorry schleps who didn't have the good fortune or money required to live on campus. We were the locals whose parents refused to pay out-of-state tuition, room and board when "There is a perfectly good university right here." And Dad would add, "I won't pay for taking classes over two or three times, so you better pass them the first time."

There were also out-of-state students who lived in one of the many off-campus apartments. Most of them decided after their freshman year that dorm life wasn't for them. They didn't enjoy having to deal with rules like curfews, no booze, and, especially, prohibiting the commingling of males and females. Also, many dorms at UF lacked air conditioning, making life a hot, sticky mess, and the summer semester practically unbearable. The university required all students to attend at least one summer semester. Locals usually attended year-round to spread out their class loads so they could work.

Arriving at the commuter lot didn't mean you could simply park and go. There was a two-to-one ratio of demand from commuters vs. supply of parking spaces. This came straight out of Economics 101. The hunt began as I turned into the lot. The first strategic decision (Business 102) was, go down the first row and work my way out, or use reverse logic and go to the farthest point and work my back? Normal parking lot psychology says most people look for the closest spot to their destination, which in this case, was the campus bus stop at the entrance. But this wasn't normal. Locals were always pushing the time envelope by arriving with barely enough time to catch the commuter lot bus which took us up to campus.

I began spot stalking, the process of following people walking to their cars after getting off the bus. Upon pulling into the lot, I'd idle in place a couple of rows down from the entrance. This was creepy, especially for coeds, as spot stalkers would slowly follow them up and down the rows. Sometimes they tried to fake out stalkers by intentionally cutting across a row or two before heading to their cars.

Time was running out to make it to class. I'd have to park on the grass or in a reserved spot on campus and pray I didn't get a ticket or worse, towed. At the last minute, a coed put the fake on a freshman dupe. But I had experience here.

*You're not going to that big old station wagon are you, darling. No, you look more like that cute little Toyota Corolla. I'll position myself for that spot. Come on, that's it, getting closer... there she goes, right for the Corolla. Damn, I'm good at spot stalking…uh, that doesn't sound right at all! Pay attention, get up there, and put your blinker on or you'll lose the spot.*

Whew, I whipped into the parking space, avoiding a collision with both the departing coed and another oncoming commuter. I had only seconds to sprint across the frying pan of asphalt to the bus stop.

The burning sun melted the tar in the asphalt, causing it to ooze up through cracks in the pavement and stick to the bottoms of my shoes. If you missed the bus you were in for one hellacious half mile uphill run, with a backpack full of huge textbooks, notebooks, pens, pencils and the ubiquitous TI (Texas Instruments) calculator. Unless you were an engineering student, in which case it was the ubiquitous HP40C. There was nothing like sitting down in an ice-cold lecture hall, soaked in sweat, and dripping all over your notes, resulting in a smeared, illegible mess, all while attempting to not stare at the nipple forest.

*Wow, I copped a parking space and made the bus on the first try! Must be my lucky day.*

The ride up through campus was usually quiet as none of us really knew anyone else on the bus. A few students crammed for an exam or were desperate to finish an assignment before class. I preferred to look out the window and watch all the students buzzing about. UF is a very large campus. Freshman classes were spread out all over the place, leaving little time to hustle from one class to the next.

The commuter bus dropped us off in a central location next to General Purpose Building A. It was too new for some rich old alumni to make a ridiculously large vanity donation and have it named after him. We called it GPA as that's how it appeared on our class schedules. Exiting the bus, we dispersed in all directions and headed to our classes. I tried to blend in—to be part of the whole campus scene. Even if only for the few hours of classes, it was my time to leave home too. To be a part of something new and distant—to have an adventure.

# 7

# HELGI

The next day was a Tuesday. I had classes on Monday, Wednesday and Friday, leaving time for a full list of chores from Dad beginning with the pool. With Hester there during the week, I didn't need to help with the rooms, and it was better to clean the pool before the guests came out. We didn't want them to see all the strong chemicals we had to put in the water. So harsh, the manufacturer advised not to get in the water for at least two hours or risk looking like a spotted lobster. Cleaning the pool involved netting out leaves dropped from the surrounding magnolias, vacuuming the bottom, brushing the side with a wide, wire brush on a long pole, and backwashing the filter.

Wearing only my micro running shorts, no shoes and no shirt, I worked my way around the pool deck. An older lady sauntered out to the pool. I didn't recall checking her in, so she probably arrived while I was in class. She took her time laying the towel over a chaise lounge at the opposite end of the pool from where I was working. Bending over she elaborately undulated her wrinkled rear in my direction.

*Eww!*

I continued working my way around the pool, keeping a watchful eye on her as I thrust the pole up and down, occasionally taking short breaks to stand and wipe the sweat from my eyes. She began rubbing suntan lotion all over her body. Cleary, she had spent way too much time in the sun. Her skin looked like cracked leather. Heavy scents of coconut oil floated over the pool, smothering my nose. I gagged. Continuing up over her shoulders and then briefly down her chest, she covered the exposed portion of her sagging boobs. She moved like a predator, hungry for a little pool-boy snack. Lying back on the chaise with one leg slightly bent, she applied some deep red lipstick, smacking her lips while eyeing me from top to bottom. I felt like fresh meat in a lion's den. My gut told me to reverse direction, but I had already brushed the other sides. The only wall left was next to Leather Lady.

*Shit, what am I going to do if she talks to me? Wants me to lotion her back or something?*

As I rounded the corner she sat up and asked, "Young man, would you be kind and put some suntan lotion on my back?"

"Um, me?" I said, as if there were someone else at the pool.

"Yes, if you wouldn't mind," she purred batting her eyelashes.

"Um…I've been working with pool chemicals ma'am. The health department prohibits me from touching anyone while cleaning the pool. It wouldn't be safe for you." It was a lie, but the only thing I could think of at the time. Never mind I wasn't wearing rubber gloves or any protective clothing.

"Oh, I'm sorry to hear that," she said. She either bought my excuse or chose to let go of her prey.

I slipped down to the pump room, out of sight. Underground, in the small, dank, concrete room canisters, bags, and jugs of nasty pool stuff surrounded me. I wondered if she might follow and trap me. No one would see us or hear my screams for help over the pump. Breathing deep, the chlorine-filled air burned my lungs. Like smelling salts, it brought me back to my senses. I remembered the explicit warnings from the previous owner of the motel never to mix the chlorine with the pool acid. The resulting cloud of gas could kill you. I was caught between chemical or bikini-flab asphyxiation.

A few minutes of breathing the noxious fumes of the pump room forced me back out for some fresh air. I emerged to find that Leather Lady had returned to her room. Relieved to be out of the awkward situation, anger and frustration took over. I couldn't even get one college coed on campus to acknowledge my existence, but a wrinkled old lady wearing a bikini comes on to me in broad daylight at a fleabag motel.

*What the hell is wrong with me? It's gotta be this damn motel!*

# 8

# HELGI

On the ride up through campus, a girl at the front of the bus caught my eye. Most of the coeds lived on campus and many were from out of state. Her look, the clothes she wore, and that she was on the commuter lot bus, told me she was likely part of the indigenous population—a local. Parted down the middle, her silky light brown hair flowed softly over her shoulders. Her creamy smooth skin was light for a native Floridian. Wearing a simple, loose-fitting white blouse and high-waist blue jeans, she appeared unpretentious. In fact, she appeared quite at ease, serene, yet focused. When the bus arrived at the campus stop, she stood to get off the bus. Tall and slender, she had long legs that "went right up to heaven," as Dad would say with a grin and a wink. It had taken until my late teens to figure out what he meant.

As she turned to exit the bus, our eyes connected. Oh, what beautiful eyes! They instantly pierced my soul. Her face was welcoming in an "I like you" manner. Like

Bambi, who sees girl—no—*the* girl for the first time, I was "twitterpated!"

I had to meet her, but how? Spot stalking her in the commuter lot was probably a bad idea and only slightly creepier than following her to class. The bus let us off in the center of campus next to General Purpose Building A. The business school was located on the northeast corner of campus, so I had to go right. Unfortunately, Commuter Girl headed in the opposite direction down Stadium Road.

Hmm, that can only mean one of three schools, engineering, computer science or journalism. I thought she must be super-smart, a computer geek or an aspiring journalist, dreaming of a head-anchor job on the nightly news. Her appearance, plain beauty and calm demeanor told me she was too nice, honest and genuine to be in journalism. I ran into those pukes in English classes. They were pushy, rude and arrogant. So, that left computer science or engineering.

I glanced down at my watch.

*Gotta go; I'm going to be late for class. I hope I run into her again.*

# 9

# KRISTINA

Kristina Schmitt boarded the commuter bus. Taking a seat near the front, she noticed a guy in the back. Not one to pay attention to the opposite sex, she was surprised by the sudden rush of excitement coursing through her veins. A no-nonsense, hard-working freshman, she loved to study, especially math. Determined to graduate early and with straight As, she had planned each class for every semester right up to graduation. College would see her bloom from curious student to a well-versed engineering grad at the top of her class, ready to make her mark as a professional engineer. What she didn't plan on was falling in love. Boys weren't a part of the equation. A late bloomer with a strict Catholic upbringing, she had yet to have a serious boyfriend, but that was all about to change. More importantly, she was about to discover things about herself she never knew existed and it had all been set into motion with a glance and a smile she gave a boy on the bus.

When the bus stopped to let them off in the middle

of campus, for some unknown reason she turned to check him out one more time. Their eyes met. He smiled at her. She smiled back. Something stirred in the pit of her stomach.

A little flustered by the encounter, Kristina headed down Stadium Road to the College of Engineering building.

*He was cute. Why did I smile at him?*

# 10

# HELGI

Back at the asylum...err...motel, the day appeared normal.

"Hey Mom, did Dad get back yet?" I asked as I entered the office. "What's the status of the loon in number nine?"

"Well, he stopped ringing the front desk, and Hester got in his room for a stay-over service. Don't know if he was there or not," Mom said while flipping through receipts on the counter.

"Stay over! Are you kidding me? You guys didn't give him the boot AND you let Hester go in his room… alone?" I sounded off.

"He paid for two days up front and said he might stay longer."

"Oh, sure, that makes it all right...are you crazy?"

"Settle down, Helgi, Dad's not concerned. Besides, he keeps the .38 behind the front desk."

"Yeah, but it's for self-defense, and, *besides*, we don't go walking around with it in plain sight," I countered.

"What's your point?" Mom asked.

"What's my point? Aargh!"

"Your dad will keep an eye on him and, if he tries anything, he'll toss him out on his ear."

That I believed. The Old Man was built like a brick shit house, about as wide as he was tall and nothing but lean, solid muscle. When threatened, he'd put on a Clint Eastwood go-ahead-make-my-day look that would scare the crap out of anyone. You didn't want to be on the receiving end of a pissed-off Sven.

Dad told me a story from his high school days. Some tough guys said they were going to beat him up after school. When his last class let out, he moseyed down to the nearby soda fountain, where the fight would take place, sat down at the counter and enjoyed a strawberry shake. All the time knowing the so-called tough guys were waiting for him outside.

Sven finished his shake, paid the check, walked out the door to the leader of the pack and dropped him with one uppercut to the chin. Then he turned to the others and said, "Who's next?" They all ran away faster than a herd of sheep chased by a wolf. Dad was a badass, but only when necessary. Otherwise, he was a quiet, hard-working guy. If he was ok with "Number Nine" staying over, I was ok...as long as I didn't have to go over there again.

"What's up for this weekend?" I asked. "Did the band check in yet?"

"They arrived while you were on campus this afternoon."

# 11

# HELGI

The band was a rock group that played local nightclubs. They looked and sounded like Loggins and Messina with some Carly Simon in the mix. All of them sported shoulder-length hair, both the guys and the girls, and donned newer, cleaner versions of Woodstock garb. A few of them were couples, but the pairings changed from visit to visit.

The consensus from my parents who went to hear them play was "they're pretty good." You'd think it would have been me going out on the town at eighteen. But no, they left me to man the front desk while my parents went out for a few bumps and some dancing. Sven and Leena were very social and loved to party and dance.

I must have been some sort of throwback, as I was content taking the slow, after-dinner shift to check in a few late arrivals. I could get in some quiet study time as well.

The living quarters were adjacent to the office and

directly connected by a doorway behind the front desk. Getting a snack from the kitchen or hitting the bathroom when nature called was only a few steps away. Trust me there were nights no one pulled in, and the switchboard never rang.

It was a double-edged sword when the band came to town. The upside for me was the female members. They would sunbathe by the pool all day in bikinis, and yes, they were worthy of wearing them. It's funny how the pool always needed cleaning when the band girls were there. Sporting my pool cleaning uniform, micro-thin running shorts split up the sides of my legs, no shirt, and breaking a good sweat while doing my best imitation of The Hoff, I strutted around the pool like a Peacock in matting season. Unfortunately, they didn't notice me—unless they wanted more towels. The guys usually rolled out of the sack at noon grabbed some cold, leftover pizza from a box sitting on a nightstand, light up a joint and watched TV.

We always put the band in adjoining rooms seventeen and eighteen, which became one huge, messy lair for hanging out between shows. That was the other edge of the sword. They were pigs! Cleaning their rooms for the stay-over nights, let alone when they finally checked out was a friggin' nightmare. The ash trays were mounded with butts and ashes. Filthy wet towels and washcloths cluttered the two rooms. Trash cans overflowed with old food, potato chip bags and beer cans. Used condom foils were hidden in places I didn't know existed, but I had to find-em to toss-em. It was like a gross Easter egg hunt. An acrid combination of cigarette smoke, pot, incense, old pizza and B.O. lingered in the rooms. I swear I could see the air when I entered. It took me the same time to clean the band's rooms as it did for three full checkouts. But they were good customers, who paid in cash, never haggled over our rates and returned to our little motel every time they came to town. So, we were all too happy to take their money and clean their mess.

# 12

# HELGI

Settling in for a quiet evening, the sun shot a last blast of heat over the motel and sunk out of sight. As day became night, I flipped switches in the office to turn on the outside lights, illuminating the walkways, parking lot and our beloved sign. The white neon VACANCY boldly announced we had rooms available. I would turn on the NO when it was time to close and watch *Saturday Night Live*. Two banks of fluorescents in the office lit up everything like a Broadway marquee. If someone tried to rob us, at least witnesses could give a good description of the perps. The previous owner drilled into us, when the lights go on, the office door gets locked—no exceptions. This would ultimately prove to be life-saving advice. But, for the moment it was me, calculus and the motel.

In the morning, I'd start cleaning rooms closest to the road as the band slept. They returned around 2 a.m. after each performance. I knew this because my bedroom in the living quarters was next to theirs. They were amped up after each show and partied until three or four in the morning. Since we didn't have Nooners on the weekends, those patrons were home with their actual spouses, there was no rush to get vacancies ready before midafternoon.

# 13

# HELGI

Working my way down the row of rooms on Fogman's side of the motel, I again heard the faint chant of "number nine, number nine, number nine…". Harmless, but it still sent chills up my spine.

*Geesh, is he ever going to stop this shit?*

I thought about forgetting to stop at his room. If the cart would cooperate and not sound like a Sherman tank passing by.... *Damn.* The door started to open. He was looking right at me.

*Crap. Why me?*

"Good morning fog...um...sir. Do you need room service today?" I said with a *please god, say no* inflection.

I kept rolling the cart, praying I didn't have to stop. Meanwhile, Fogman stared at me without moving out of the way to allow me in the room. He stood there silently, not even chanting. His cold eyes pierced through me as if I wasn't there.

Again, I nervously asked if I could clean his room as I continued pushing the cart past his door. His head turned, following me as I passed by. His eyes never flinched. I stared back, feeling both chilled and a bit pissed-off. As the distance between us grew, he slowly closed the room door at the same speed I was pushing the cart...slowly, very slowly.

Now there had been two face-to-face encounters with Fogman and this time both Mom and Dad were nowhere in sight or screaming distance. I went to the office for a bathroom break which made no sense as there were toilets in every room. But I needed to get away from Number Nine to calm my nerves and report the latest incident to management. The folks were having some lunch, while Grandma manned the front desk and worked on the books.

"Hi Grandma, what're you up to?"

"Recording expenses for all the things Leena bought from that nice salesman."

If I had any sense at all I'd have sat down with the only person in the family with a post high school education and learned about the ledger sheets, credits and debits. It might have helped me understand Accounting 101.

Grandma was impressive. The daughter of first-generation immigrants from Finland who didn't speak English. Her bookkeeping education wasn't about women's suffrage. It was about financial survival, pure and simple. Grampa died at a young age, leaving her alone with Leena. Instead of looking for another husband to support them, she went to bookkeeping classes, got her certificate and found a job.

Grandma was the nicest, most gentle, never-had-anything-bad-to-say person you could ever meet. Whatever life threw at her, she would always say, "It's good that happened." Meaning bad things happen for a reason and would lead to something good.

"Hey guys, saw our friend in number nine again," I reported. "He was staring out his door but didn't respond when I asked if he wanted room service. I hope like hell he checks out in the morning."

"Ok thanks, are all the rooms done?" Mom bellowed from the kitchen.

"No, I'm half done. It's not even noon yet, but thanks for your concern about my well-being."

"When you're done with the rooms, the lawn needs mowing," Dad added.

"Roger that."

Fridays meant more check-outs than check-ins. Unless it was a football weekend, we typically had about half the rooms to clean. That's why we only had Hester work Monday to Friday. There wasn't enough work to make it worth her while and *management* saved a few bucks as they didn't have to pay me as much.

It looked like I would get the rooms done by noon, which left time to mow the lawn and study.

*I wonder if Commuter Girl goes to the library on Saturdays.*

# 14

# HELGI

Locals had real lives with jobs and responsibilities. We didn't live the artificial life of the campus crowd. On the other hand, frats and dorm rats lived the campus life. They started their academic week with good intentions by going to class and stopping by the library—where they made plans to party. The next day they would oversleep, miss morning classes, but somehow pulled it together for an afternoon elective in art or rocks for jocks. Then they began drinking again on the theory that the earlier they started, the earlier they would pass out—thus getting a full night's sleep and make it to class on time the next morning. Let's just say, the multiple trials conducted to prove their thesis usually resulted in waking up next to a stranger or hung over with their head firmly planted on the floor next to the toilet.

I don't know how they passed any classes, let alone graduated at the end of four years. But most of them were on the new college calendar. You know, get a four-year degree in only five short years! But don't worry, little frat boy. When you eventually do graduate, Daddy will get you a nice cushy position in his firm or connect you with one of his frat brothers, who will give you a job. You'll collect a generous paycheck with bennies, still be able to party, albeit only on the weekends, and get your picture in the alumni magazine for a big promotion at the company. Of course, you won't have to report to work until after spending a year abroad to "find yourself." Again, paid for by Daddy!

Locals hated the frats. We saw them as spoiled little brats who came to *our* town and *our* university and acted like they owned the place. Worse, they had the audacity and arrogance to decided who was good enough to join their elite little club. I went to one rush party to pledge a frat thinking it was a path to normal and away from the motel. Everything I thought about them as a local was reinforced by what I witnessed. Beer bongs, real bongs, groping coeds, puking in the bushes, all while dressed in khakis and button-down dress shirts. Dickheads all. And that damn music they blared—Devo, Kiss and Queen. Didn't they know this was Jimmy Buffet country?

Kappa Kappa my ass. Kappa Kappa Dickheads was more like it.

I wasn't a prude by any stretch of the imagination, but their privileged presence on campus combined with the reality of my own situation pissed me off. I thought I wanted to trade places with one of those privileged pukes, but I didn't fit in…with the frats or the motel.

I finished up the rooms, loaded the laundry and hopped on the ancient riding mower. Hot is hot, sweaty is sweaty, so multi-tasking was the order of the day. I needed to get everything done by early afternoon to have a chance of running into Commuter Girl at the library. Assuming she was even there.

I knew exactly how much grass to cut before the laundry had to be switched from washer to dryer and then hop back on the mower. Once done with everything, I headed straight to the pool. Dripping with sweat from head to toe, guests or no guests, I jumped right in with all my clothes. Never gave it much thought, but it probably grossed out the moms while little Johnny and Suzy played in the shallow end.

Sinking to the cool water of the deep end, I'd lay on the bottom like a manatee. I could feel the heat radiating away from me into the water. The huge commercial pump put out so much pressure it created a current which flowed over my baked body. My shoulder-length hair swayed back and forth like seaweed on the ocean floor. For a few brief moments, I was in a state of suspended animation, no sound, no parents, no motel and no "number nine."

*Econ exam next week, need to study. Fogman…why me? Ah Commuter Girl.*

While I meditated at the bottom, I imagined the guests relaxing in the loungers wondered if I was ok.

*"Do you think he drowned?" A lady nervously asks her husband. "Should we call someone?"*

My lungs told my brain "Hello, running out of oxygen, must breathe." I tucked my legs to my chest and pushed off the bottom. Surfacing like a breaching whale, I gasped in deep breath of air and climbed out the side in one, continuous motion. Water puddled at my feet as I drip dried before the unnerved guests. Chores completed; I could go to the library.

# 15

# HELGI

UF had massive old libraries. Built of stone, with ornate arched entrances, they rose like cathedrals, anchoring the university to its founding roots. On the main level were cavernous halls with large, heavy tables. Overbuilt from solid oak, they could accommodate eight to ten students with plenty of room for their textbooks and notepads. The walls were lined with magnificent floor-to-ceiling bookshelves that loomed overhead like sentries. Countless volumes comprising a repository of infinite wisdom overwhelmed my senses. At times, I would stand before this holy grail of words and wonder what was in all those tomes. Cracked bindings precariously held together millions of yellowing pages. Fading covers surrounded their essence as a mother embraces a child.

I wondered if anyone had ever read them all. How long had it been since they were picked up? When was the last time they were checked out? I felt bad for them. Maybe they weren't looking down their long spines at us from lofty shelves. Instead they were begging for someone —anyone—to take them down, open them up and read their stories. If you preferred more seclusion, you could go up into the Stacks. Located on the uppermost floors of the libraries, the Stacks were small attic-like rooms with low ceilings, so named as the books were literally stacked from floor to ceiling on old, gray, metal shelving. Bastards to the prestigious bookcases surrounding the grand halls below, the Stacks were the orphanage for old, frayed and neglected books.

You accessed the Stacks via ever-narrowing staircases with marble steps so worn they were noticeably thinner at their centers. A single, tiny elevator barely held two people. If you were the least bit claustrophobic, the stairs were your only option. In addition to the tight rows of bookshelves undersized desks hugged the walls. A few sat alone under hazy windows. Students tossed books haphazardly without a care for Dewey Decimal. The stale air smelled musty from the old, leather covers. Overtaken by a forest of metal shelves, the Stacks were the final resting place for obsolete books. Discarded and forgotten to the library's cemetery.

The space had the eerie feel of a haunted house. So quiet, the words from my textbooks shouted off the pages and echoed in my head. So isolated, I could sense all who had been there before me—of all who toiled over their work late into the night. Often by myself, I never felt alone in the Stacks. No one ever bothered me up there. This is where I would go to study and to get away from the motel. This is where I found some peace of mind.

# 16

# HELGI

It was Saturday afternoon when I entered the library. The grand hall was nearly empty. Normally I'd head up to the Stacks. The comings and goings of fellow students were a distraction, let alone the incessant whispering of a few rude idiots.

Glancing over the tables on my way to the stairs, long, straight hair flowing down a slender, tall back of a female student caught my eye. I froze in my tracks. It was her…Commuter Girl!

Instantly, I changed course from the Stacks to the grand hall and walked toward her. Like a magnet held in front of a compass, her presence pulled me forward. Books in hand, heart in throat, I made my way over to her table.

*Don't sit too close. Don't want to scare her away.*

I pushed hard against the magnetism and sat a few seats from her on the opposite side of the table. Being a lefty, I arranged my books to my right and notepads to the left. This helped matters as Commuter Girl was to my right. I could steal a peek while looking up from my textbooks.

*Look, don't stare!*

BAM! Her image smacked my heart, sending shivers down my spine…awakening something I'd never felt before.

*My God, she's more beautiful than the first time I saw her on the bus.*

Difficult as it was, I tried to keep my eyes on my opened books. I made some notes to blend in with other students, who scribbled into their notebooks. To move into glancing position, I highlighted in my econ textbook. As the yellow marker glided over the page, left to right, back and forth, my eyes drifted past the page and over to her. Another glimpse, another palpitation. This sequence continued until reality crept into my head.

*I can't study. What to do, what to do?* I turned the page—notes, highlight, glance. *Oh shit, she's looking at me. Busted. Did she …?*

Commuter Girl shot back the same smile she'd given me the first time our eyes met on the bus. Whatever my expression, it was involuntary and unedited. I prayed it wasn't creepy or pathetic. At least she didn't recoil in pain and horror. She held her stare for a precious second or two and then returned to her studies.

I had to think through my strategy. The next step. Since I came in after her, I couldn't be the first to leave, lest my short study session be revealed for what it was, a way to meet her.

I didn't want to be just another guy coming on to her, and having no experience in this arena, any attempt would likely end up poorly. Besides, my feelings were poking at the synapse in my brain. This was way more than simple lust. This was something else. While driving with coeds made me horny, for some crazy reason sex hadn't crossed my mind. Every emotion I was experiencing was in my head and my heart. There was nothing going on below the belt. This was uncharted territory. I didn't understand what was happening to me.

*God, those eyes! How am I going to break the ice? Does she know I'm a local? Will it matter to her?*

The local girls usually wanted to meet someone from out of state. New blood for the gene pool. I blamed Darwin for stacking the cards against us hometown boys. Well, at least that was my excuse.

Our eyes met for a third time that glorious Saturday afternoon. Both of us were playing the study-lookup game. If her smile said, "I like you." Then mine said, "I love you. I want to marry you and make babies."

*Whoa, too much! Turn down the volume a couple of levels, boy, or this will be the last time you see her.*

Too late. My heart-on-my-sleeve look was already on its way. Like regretful words that fly out of your mouth with no way to get them back, my expression, complete with a proposal of marriage, flew across the table and landed right on target.

*Oh crap. How did it hit? Was it like a love bug splatting on a car windshield, making a mess of everything or did it settle in the soft embrace of her acceptance?*

The study-lookup game continued a few more rounds until it was uncomfortably clear someone had to do something, or this would get weird. She began to close her books and carefully put them into her backpack. Standing up, she glanced at me and smiled. I smiled back. We made eye contact. Commuter Girl turned and walked down the aisle between the tables of the grand hall, her long hair waving from side to side as if to say, "This was nice, let's do it again sometime."

Mesmerized, I watched her disappear through the entrance. Feelings of exhilaration and desire gripped every fiber of my body. I couldn't move. Distracted by my reaction to her presence, I never looked at her textbooks. That would have been helpful to know what school she was in.

I didn't get her name. I didn't talk to her—didn't hear her voice.

*Will I see her again?*

# 17

# KRISTINA

Kristina couldn't believe she had run into Bus Boy again. Surprised by the butterflies in her stomach, she didn't understand what she was experiencing at the sight of him. It was confusing, but she liked it. Inexperienced with boys, she wanted to meet him but didn't know how. The thought of talking to him never crossed her mind. She wasn't sure what to do. Should she say something? Break the ice?

*He must be shy. I wonder if he always comes to the library to study.*

Distracted by his presence and those darn butterflies, she decided to shuffle her notes and steal a glance or two. Her heart skipped when their eyes met. The palms of her hands began to sweat. Kristina couldn't focus on her assignments. This had never happened to her before. She had lost control of her feelings. Normally this would have upset her, but this time something was different. She didn't know how to process the situation.

*This is crazy. Must get to class. Okay, just one more look.*

She looked across the table. Bus Boy was looking right at her. His look penetrated her eyes and shot straight into her heart. Heat boiled up from deep inside her body—from a place she never knew existed. Kristina froze.

*Oh…my…what is hap…I can't breathe!*

Overwhelmed by her emotions, she closed her books, picked up her backpack and stood up to leave. Once again, forces beyond her understanding took over as she warmly smiled at Bus Boy. More than a mere glance, she returned a warm, endearing smile at him. She wanted to say something, but didn't know what or how, so she slowly turned and walked away.

Kristina Schmitt uncharacteristically beamed as she practically skipped through campus.

# 18

# HELGI

Another sleepy Saturday evening at the motel. A few guests were milling about: some lounged by the pool. Traffic was quieter than usual. The summer heat abated as the broiling sun disappeared behind a stand of ancient live oaks. Dusk evaporated into night. With the flick of a few switches, the lights illuminated the motel and our neon sign pointed out the entrance. The office lights spilled over the parking lot giving the place a sense of life. The Florida Motel appeared like a desert oasis from the road.

The folks watched TV in the living quarters while I manned the desk. I had no sooner cracked my econ textbook when something caught my eye. Some sort of commotion out by number eight. A couple had checked in earlier in the day. Both in their twenties, he was a tall, strapping guy with black, well-styled hair and nicely tanned skin. Looked like a GQ model. Almost too perfect. She was petite with long blond hair, firm body and absolutely rocked her bikini earlier at the pool. They had been in number eight for a while when without warning, the woman burst out of their room and frantically ran toward the office screaming, "Help me! Help me!"

She was stark naked!

With not a stitch on her beautiful, young body, she ran like a crazy person down the middle of the parking lot. Boobs-a-jiggling, hair-a-flying, a full-frontal nude lady charged right at me. An actual naked woman—not a magazine centerfold precariously held by one hand. My eyes bulged out of my head. Another bulge formed in my jeans. This was way better than *Playboy*.

Hey, I was concerned for her safety, but I was still the same eighteen-year-old guy distracted by scantily clad campus coeds. No matter, I could multitask.

"Ah…Ma…Da…Dad?"

"What do you need, Helgi?" Mom said over Archie Bunker's ongoing fight with Meathead.

"Umm…there's…ahh…there's a naked lady at outside."

Dad was off the couch and into the office faster than…dare I say…a speeding bullet.

"Help me! Help me!" she screamed while banging on the door.

"Don't open it," Mom ordered.

"What the hell? She needs help!" I pleaded to no avail.

Clearly, Mom didn't want Dad protecting a drop-dead-gorgeous, twenty-something, naked woman. Besides, we never unlocked the front door after sunset. You never knew what the real deal was when crazy shit like this happened in the motel biz. We were also not on the best side of Gainesville, not the worst, but still sketchy, especially after dark. She could have been strung-out on drugs or this could have been a distraction for a robbery.

"Helgi, call the police," Mom commanded as she positioned herself between Dad and me.

For chrissake, a beautiful, young, naked woman stood banging on the office door and my mother was blocking the view. This could only happen to me.

"What's the matter?" Dad asked while looking her over. "What's going on?"

"Stop staring, Sven." Mom snarled.

"Leena, I'm yust making sure she's not hurt," he replied defensively.

"Help, he's trying to beat me!"

The mood turned serious. All jean-bulging, horny thoughts running through me came crashing *down.* I immediately donned the switchboard headset, plugged in the kraken to get an outside line and dialed 911. Nut cases and motel craziness is one thing, but violence is scary. Guess Mom's instincts were right.

"Calm down, miss. Come around to da night vindow," Dad instructed with empathy. "Leena, get me a clean sheet from yunder da desk."

Mom quickly grabbed one for a double even though a single would have done the job. Dad pushed it out through the narrow slot. This was no small feat as it was designed to only open a few inches.

"Here, take this and wrap yourself up," he said. "No one's going to hurt you. Stay there while we wait for the police."

Naked Lady now looked as though she had come

from a toga party on campus. Her screams for help melted into sobbing. Tears streamed down her distraught face and dripped onto her chest. Mixing with the sweat beading off her hot body, they flowed like a river passing between her mountainous breasts. Her wet skin glistened under the office light. The boyfriend pursued her into the parking lot but stopped when he saw us in the office. He quickly returned to their room and shut the door.

The phone line crackled alive in the headset.

"Nine one one, what's your emergency?"

"A-a-a naked lady…"

"Excuse me, sir. There's a what?"

"Na-na-naked la-lady," I stammered.

"Sir, what is the nature of your emergency?"

I pulled myself together. "This is the Florida Motel on SW 13th Street. There's a naked lady screaming for help."

"What seems to be the problem, sir?"

"The woman is saying something about her boyfriend beating her up."

"Where is she now, sir?" the operator asked.

"She's outside the office. Mom wouldn't let her in. Dad is trying to help her," I responded.

"Help her how? I thought you said she was outside?"

"She is."

"Naked?"

"Not anymore."

"Sir, how is she not naked if you won't let her in?"

"Hey, I wanted to let her in! It's Leena's fault."

"Who is Leena, sir?" the emergency operator asked.

"My mother…ma'am," I said with a snarky tone.

"Oh, I see. Your mother, Leena, doesn't want to let a

screaming naked lady into the office with her husband and son. Is that correct, sir?"

"Correct, but my dad gave her a sheet to cover up with."

"I thought the naked lady was locked outside the office?"

"She is."

"Then how did she get the sheet?"

"The Old Man…I mean, my dad, pushed it through the slot in the night window"

"Oh, I see. We have a unit on the way."

Two police cars pulled in while I was still on the phone with the 911 operator. Their flashing lights on, but no siren. These disturbance calls were all too common at these little motels.

"The police are here," I reported to the operator.

"Ok, I'll hang up. The officers will take over from here."

"Thank you…*ma'am*." I replied, while getting back to observing the situation.

"Go inside Helgi," Mom ordered. "We'll handle this,"

I don't know if it was her protective motherly instincts kicking in or not wanting me to see any more of our guest than I already had, but I wasn't leaving the scene of *this* crime. No way, no how!

"That's okay, Ma. I'll stay here at the front desk."

"I really think…"

"Hey, if I have to deal with the nut case in number nine and deliver unwanted towels to Nooners, then I can be here for this," I argued, cutting her off.

She didn't have a good comeback for that one. Mom

was too busy keeping an eye on Dad, who kept both eyes on Naked Lady. This was a historic event. I had finally won an argument with my stubborn Finn mother. It wouldn't be repeated anytime soon…if ever.

The cops went about their business, ignoring our banter. By now, practically every guest was peering out their windows or standing in doorways taking in the spectacle. The Mrs. in a family from the Midwest, with her pinched features and shaking head, was aghast at the unseemly sight. Wide-eyed and slack-jawed, Mr. stood there like he was witnessing the second coming. A frantic mother at the window of another room tried to cover little Johnny's eyes to no avail. Squirming free, he was determined to see what was going on. The salesman from New Jersey reacted as if it were another normal day back home.

One of the officers interviewed Naked Lady while the other lumbered to room eight to question the boyfriend. To them, this was just another fender bender with a lot of paperwork. Once the gravity of law enforcement's presence sunk in, Naked Lady's claims of abuse diminished to a lover's quarrel.

*If that's a quarrel, I can't wait to see them fight. I'll have to get some popcorn for the next show.*

Thirty minutes passed when the officers returned to get our side of the story. After the hubbub settled, they asked us what we wanted them to do. Naked Lady didn't want to press charges, and there were no physical signs of abuse, so their hands were tied.

"I vant dem outta here right now!" Mom ordered before Dad opened his mouth. He instinctively kept quiet and nodded in agreement. At that moment there was nothing he could say without serious risk to life and limb. This was dangerous territory. Didn't matter that we had two police officers there to protect us. Eventually, they would leave, and Dad and I would be left alone with Mom. She knew what her boys wanted, and we knew she knew. We also had the other guests to consider. We didn't want them to check out because of this little ruckus.

"Please escort them off the property, Officers."

"Yes, ma'am," they replied.

There would be no encore show tonight. Cancel the popcorn.

The young couple sheepishly loaded up their car and left with two of Gainesville's finest right behind. All was quiet again. The other guests returned to their rooms. The folks went back to watching TV, and I went back to studying. Another day in the life at the Florida Motel.

*I'll need a long shower tonight.*

# 19

# HELGI

"I finished rooms eight, ten and fifteen. Laundry is going. I'm off to class."

"Ok, see you later," Mom said.

There was nothing new on the wall this morning. It had been a quiet weekend on campus. The football team played an away game, and midterms were fast approaching. The student body must have sobered up to concentrate on maintaining their C averages. Dorm rats and Frats put in just enough effort to avoid academic trouble, but not enough to waste energy on needless studies. Hopefully, that didn't apply to the pre-med and nuclear engineering students. I really wanted them to get straight A's.

Turning off Museum Road to the commuter lot, I realized there weren't any coeds strutting about. Funny, no Driving with Coeds today. *Good grief, were they actually studying?*

Turned out they were still there, but I didn't notice them. Either there was something wrong with my vision or they couldn't compete with Naked Lady. Nope, she wasn't on my mind either and I could clearly see "Commuter Parking Lot" on the approaching bus. Crazy, instead of butts-n-boobs I was thinking about buses—and their passengers. *Would she be on the bus today?*

Wasting no time, I boarded and took a seat in the back. That way I could look at her without creeping her out. Scanning the lot, there was no sight of her. Other students hastily parked, and jogged over to catch the bus, but no Commuter Girl.

Right on schedule, and without mercy, the driver closed the door and pulled away. Panic-stricken faces could be seen all over the lot as late-arriving locals realized they missed the bus and now had to make the long, hot walk up the hill to campus. They were doomed to daylong sweaty wedgies.

The commuter bus pulled up to GPA, followed by the married housing bus. UF had several married housing complexes on campus. They were primarily for post-graduate students working on their MBA's or Ph.D.'s. They too wanted to blend in, especially the guys when they were around the coeds. But unlike the young undergrads, they stuck out like dull, drab weeds in a field of delicate wildflowers. Wearing dowdy clothes, the guys had the beginnings of a pot bellies from eating cheap, generic macaroni and cheese five days a week. It was all they could afford. Many of the wives were pregnant or had already given birth to a baby Gator. Their tight-fitting jeans didn't complement their post-pregnancy figures. Some simply gave up and tossed on sail-sized sun dresses. As the married housing students got off their special bus, the undergrads would spread apart like they were avoiding the plague. Coeds, frats and dorm rats all moved out of the way and never made eye contact with them for fear of turning into salt or contracting the dreaded marriage disease. It was bad enough being a local. I couldn't imagine being a married local. That would be as bad as living and working at the Florida Motel. I quickly fled from both buses. In a few short steps, I was once again part of the *normal* student body heading to class.

As the day proceeded, I looked everywhere for Commuter Girl, down every sidewalk, between every building and I checked the libraries. Nothing.

At noon, I made my way over to the Plaza of the Americas. It was an open lawn canopied by live oaks covered in Spanish moss. The huge trees were like umbrellas for the sun. Surrounded by the libraries on the east and north, the bell tower to the south and dorms to the west, the plaza was a tranquil place to relax between classes.

The Krishnas were setting up for lunch. They gave away food, handed out pamphlets and chanted. Unlike "Number nine...," this chanting was easy on the ears and seemed to fit in with the whole campus vibe. They shaved their heads and wore robe-like clothing that was the same opaque color as the mush they served for lunch. It tasted like Mom's Finn cooking—bland. Their rhythmic incantation was accompanied by bongos and cymbals. Think hippies who didn't drink or do drugs. I'm not sure where they stood on free sex, but there were cute baby Krishna's in hand-woven wraps attached to their mothers. Some larger models ran around with miniature bongos and cymbals. The

Krishnas weren't preachy, didn't bother anyone and never got in your face. They were pacifists, and whoever said "there are no free lunches" had never met the Krishnas.

Sitting on the ground with my back against a century-old oak and enjoying some free mush, I took in the whole scene. Lunch on the Plaza was like studying in the Stacks…peaceful. I thought about Commuter Girl.

Then my mind wandered. How did the university come up with core classes for majors? I could understand taking economics, marketing, and finance for a business degree, but calculus? Really? What the hell did that have to do with learning business? Management Information Systems (MIS) was another one. It made sense from the description in the course catalog but unfortunately turned out to be a computer programming class. They probably needed more students signed up to cover the cost of the big mainframe computer used for research. I imagined the university's leadership running through the annual budget.

President: "We don't have enough computer geeks to pay for the IBM mainframe."

Bean counter: "Hey, why not make Programming 101 a core requisite for the business majors? We have a ton of them enrolled. We'll put the word 'management' in the title and course description."

President: "I like it. Make it happen."

Personally, I didn't need to know how a computer worked or how to write a program. I only needed it to spit out answers to questions. Businesspeople hire geeks to figure out the other stuff. But the argument was in my head and as effective as that stupid tree falling in a forest with no one around. So, I bit the bullet and registered for MIS 101. Best to get it out of the way.

I set out to the computer lab to test drive a punch card thingy and its brother the card reader. My textbook talked about FORTRAN or COBOL. Language only engineers and research scientists would ever use, it all sounded like some COBOLTRAN shit to me.

The assignment was to write a program and then convert it into punch cards that the mainframe would run when they were fed through the reader. The card reader looked like a money counting machine at the bank. A program consisted of a bunch of "if then" commands that resembled an electrical schematic for your TV. Program written, you placed the blank cards into the punch card thingy, typed each command into the keyboard, which then punched holes into the right spot on each card. Take the pile of cards, feed them into the reader and hit the start button. If all went according to plan, the punch cards came out the other side and, God willing, the correct result would spew out of a big, noisy printer named DOT. The cards had to be in the exact, right order and if you were missing one or mistyped even one command in the punch thingy, DOT would stop with an obnoxious ERROR—the last word you saw on the printout. Miss a comma—ERROR. Miss a space—ERROR. Worst of all, if you dropped them on the floor, you were screwed. You should've seen the look of abject horror on the faces of the engineering majors when they accidentally bumped into each other and dropped their skyscraper-high piles of cards all over the floor. One night an Asian student nudged the corner of a desk. Thousands of punch cards scattered over the lab floor. I thought he was going to commit hara-kiri right on the spot. No one and I mean no one got their program right the first time. Even without the occasional spill, it took several attempts before finally getting DOT to poop out the right answer.

The class started off with simple programs like two plus two equals four then progressed to more complex equations with hundreds of cards. It was a painstaking process that took hours to complete. To further complicate things, I took Shop instead of typing in high school. So, I had to hunt and peck the punch thingy keyboard. The printout had to be handed in as physical proof that you completed the assignment.

Late one night in the lab, I headed over to the large trash bin next to DOT to toss out, yet, another failed attempt at the mid semester assignment. This one was hard, and I was getting frustrated and stressed. I had to pass this stupid class. Hovering over the bin I had an epiphany. I could take discarded printouts of failed programs by other students and piece them together to get one entirely correct program. I knew how to punch cards for each command. What I needed were the right commands in the correct sequence. The longer the printout the more that student got right. I could do a quick quality check by comparing different programs for the same assignment. It didn't take a genius (I qualified as *not* a genius) to figure out that everyone didn't make the same mistakes, and they all stopped with that damn ERROR message. I collected multiple attempts from the trash bin. MIS101 programs were easy to spot as they were much shorter than the computer science or engineering assignments and the lines of commands looked comparatively simple. Also, the sheer volume of 101 printouts far outnumbered all others due to the university's conscription of us business majors into the class.

Of course, I'd need to be careful not to get caught as technically this was cheating. Personally, I saw it as a creative solution to a business problem utilizing the resources on hand. To improve my odds of success, I liberated all relevant printouts from the trash, neatly folded them up, stuffed them into my backpack and calmly left the computer lab.

The Stacks were the best place I could go for privacy. Couldn't risk being seen by a goodie-two-shoes student from the honors council prowling for miscreants to report to the honors council. Fortunately, these little weasels never ventured up to the Stacks. It was probably beneath them. I could've stayed up there all night, and no one would have noticed.

Pulling together the correct commands was a matter of overlapping the pages in sequence up to each error message. I laid them out side by side, kept the good pages, tore off the error pages along the perforated lines that separated each sheet, inserted the next few good pages and put them together in sequence. Ta-da, I had a complete program.

Now I could write the entire sequence in my notebook, go back to the lab, punch the cards and send them through the reader. To cover my tracks, I tossed the absconded printouts into multiple trash cans.

DOT fired up and started printing the Franken program. I held my breath as the paper spewed forth my beautiful creation. I could hear Dr. Frankenstein saying, "It's alive!" I felt both excited and relieved. Relieved that

I would get through this stupid class and excited I didn't get caught. For a split second, I was concerned that I enjoyed the thrill of it all, but it quickly passed.

My business management class covered delegation and human resources. I took what my profs had taught me and put it to practical use. Wasn't that the whole point of business school?

Mid-semester, I was again hanging out in the lab waiting for useful idiots...err... human resources, to delegate some programming for another assignment. They were so obvious when they got a program right; gleefully folding up their last printout like it was a gift on Christmas morning. DOT had given them the present they'd always wanted. I only needed their last discarded printout to get the most correct programming for each one. This meant fewer trips to the trash bin thus reducing my risk of getting caught. Straight out of Stats 101, I kept myself inside the standard deviations of the getting-busted bell curve. Although I'm sure I would've spontaneously come up with a line of BS if needed. It was also more efficient as I had fewer printouts to cut and paste. Now I was applying both Stats and Operations Management principles. There was more than one way to learn shit in college.

Sitting at one of the few small tables in the lab, I was trying to look busy with my notes and punch cards while keeping an eye on the trash, when to my surprise, in walked Commuter Girl. She sat down next to me, took out a pile of new cards from the ubiquitous oblong box we all carried around for programming, put them into the punch thingy and began working from her notes.

*Did she see me? Did she sit here on purpose?*

# 20

## HELGI

I was in a bit of a pickle. I couldn't take anything out of the trash now. Naturally I didn't want her to get the wrong impression, even though I'd completely rationalized my programming solution…at least to myself. Hey, she didn't know the printout I had wasn't mine. I could take it out and pretend I was working on my assignment. It was a solid printout from someone who appeared to be a summa cum laude candidate. Almost done, it would allow me to focus on more important tasks, like meeting Commuter Girl.

*Crap, why are there beads of sweat on my forehead? It's freezing in here!*

I needed a plan to break the ice. Dropping some of my cards on the floor between us would be too obvious. I could mumble out loud and then catch myself, feigning embarrassment as she looks over. What to do, what to do? I sneaked a peek while working out my grand plan.

Turning my head to glance over, she did the same. Our eyes met again, this time close up and personal. So close, I could smell the natural fragrance of her body. Pure and simple like a fresh ocean breeze, there wasn't any eye-burning, throat-choking Eau de Vanity from Saks Fifth Avenue emanating from this girl.

"Hey," unexpectedly came out of my mouth.

"Hi," she responded.

"Can't believe we get to have so much fun on a Saturday night," slipped out without my permission.

*Who are you and what have you done with my brain?*

"You in business too?" I asked.

"No, I'm in engineering," she said.

"Wow, you must be *really* smart."

"Not really. I just like math, especially calculus."

"You like calculus? That's crazy."

*Nice move, Slick.*

"Yeah." She shrugged. It's kinda sick."

"Can't say the same. I don't know why it's even required for business majors."

"It's really not that hard," she said with empathy.

"Well, maybe not for a genius."

*Nice recovery.*

"If I don't pass calculus, I'll have to change majors," I said.

"I'd be happy to help you sometime if you want," she offered.

"Are you sure? I mean, that would be great."

"Looks like the card reader opened up. I need to run my program."

I sat there in stunned silence as she got up and walked over to it. Like the smooth operator I was, I had forgotten to get her name, phone number or introduce myself. Her cards clattered through the reader. DOT did her thing and Commuter Girl packed up the printout. On her way out, she passed by my table.

"See you at the library sometime?" she asked.

"Sure thing," I replied, trying to play it cool.

"I'm usually there in the afternoons and sometimes on Saturdays."

"I know…I mean…yeah, sounds great."

I was struck by how easy it was to talk to her. It was like we were old friends or something.

*Did she just make a date with me?*

"Okay. Bye," she said with a gentle smile.

"Bye."

*Bye? That's it? That's all you've got? What a douchebag!*

I fumbled around with my little stack of punch cards. Trying to get back on track with Creative Programming by "Professor Pool Boy" was impossible. I should have walked out with her. Maybe offered to escort her to the commuter lot. Besides, the computer lab gave me a case of card stack envy. You see, the longer, more complex the program the more cards needed and thus the larger the stack. My business program was less than a hundred count. Commuter Girl had a medium-size pile, maybe a couple hundred or so, but the computer science majors had boxes filled with thousands of punched cards. I would've been doing well to use one box for the entire semester. They used an entire box for one program! When it came to punch cards, bigger was better…academically speaking. Walking up to the reader with my puny little stack was like getting out of a cold swimming pool wearing a speedo. Not very impressive.

# 21

# KRISTINA

Kristina was beside herself as she left the computer lab. She couldn't believe she had run into Bus Boy again, and this time they spoke to each other. *There's something special about him, but I can't put my finger on it.* She wondered if he was a local or from out of state. Unlike most of the girls in high school, Kristina was scared by the out of state guys. Too risky. Too many unknowns. Too many variables. At least local boys were all native Floridians. They had similar values and southern upbringing's, especially when it came to proper behavior and respect for ladies. And they were all fellow Gators through and through. The pragmatic scientist in her wanted to understand these new feelings. Why she couldn't concentrate on her studies when she was around him. Unfortunately, this wasn't anything she would dare look up in a textbook. Confused by these emotions, all Kristina knew for certain was she liked Bus Boy.

*My Bus Boy. Did I just ask to see him again? What's happening to me?*

# 22

# HELGI

Catching the bus at General Purpose Building A, I sat back and took in the trip to the commuter lot. Except during finals week, most days students seemed optimistic and cheerful. They had yet to be sobered up by life, work and taxes. None of them had experienced the motel biz. Did I envy them, pity them or have a leg up on them? I didn't feel one up on anyone. Hell, I was just trying to keep up.

The bus navigated Stadium Road, turned down North-South Drive, crossed Museum Road and stopped in front of the commuter lot. As I exited the bus, I spotted an old Mustang pulling out. It was a burgundy '67 coupe with black vinyl top with a 289 V8. A certified car nut, I could tell the make, model, and year with one glance.

*Nice Stang.*

An oven blast of heat hit my face when I opened my car door. Rolling down the windows, I popped in a cassette of the James Gang and cranked the volume. The tunes thumped through the 6x9 coaxial speakers as I cruised through campus back to the motel. Back to reality.

"I'm here." I surrendered coming through the door.

"Good, can you relieve grandma at the front desk?" Mom asked. "Her bunions are killing her, and I'm cooking."

We always ate dinner at six, but we didn't want to lock the office door and lose a customer. If a car pulled in, then one of us went out to register them and, hopefully, got back to the table before their food was cold.

"Hi, Grandma."

"Hi, Helgi."

"How ya doing?"

"Busy day with the books and check-ins. I need to get off my feet."

"And have a drink?" I suggested with a grin.

"If Sven makes them, I'll have one. An interesting lady checked into number sixteen."

"How so?"

"Well, her clothing is risqué, and she has on a lot of lipstick. She's also had several visitors this afternoon. Maybe she has family at the hospital."

"Is she still here?"

"No, she and her friend left a few minutes ago. They were in separate cars."

"Okay, thanks for the info. Go cop a squat and put your feet up."

Grandma moved away from the counter and slipped into the living area as I settled in for the night shift. Looking over the property from the office, I could see a family in the pool. The kids were going down the flamingo-pink slide. Several guests had pulled chairs from their rooms to sit outside as the evening heat abated to a tolerable level. Grandma's lady guest pulled up a few minutes later. She drove a beat-up old Chevy Nova, its faded brown paint worn to bare metal in places. Grandma was right. She was wearing some rather interesting threads.

*Hmmm, if I didn't know any better…*

"Dinner's ready," echoed from the kitchen.

A sliding glass partition separated the dining and living rooms. Yet another unique design feature of our little fleabag. If you didn't pay attention, or had a couple of drinks, you could walk right through it. I almost crashed through several times, sober and inebriated. I could see the headlines: "Pool boy killed tonight at the Florida Motel. According to the police he was impaled by shards of glass when he accidentally walked through a slider. Alcohol may have been a factor. Film at eleven."

"The lady in sixteen returned." I said to Grandma from the office while watching the room.

"That was quick," she replied.

Another car pulled in and parked next to the Nova. They both got out of their cars and headed to her room. He had an arm wrapped around her waist. It wasn't the same guy. She was wearing black knee-high boots, mini skirt, low cut, cleavage-exposing blouse and gobs of costume jewelry. Clearly, she didn't have family at the hospital. Nope. She was a hooker.

Hookers were okay in the motel biz. They paid in cash, never complained about the price, and were cleaner than most families. She was turning tricks and her *friends*, as Grandma noted, were the johns. She had set up shop at the Florida Motel. Must have been hooking near a bar down the road and using the motel to conduct her business.

Unlike Naked Lady, prostitutes could handle all but the most belligerent of men. They knew where to grab them to get their attention. As long as they weren't a disturbance to the other guests, we didn't care what they did and made no judgments. Everyone had to make a living, right? Still, I needed to monitor the situation. I decided to leave the room next to sixteen vacant to provide a buffer for guests during conjugal visits. We wouldn't want little Johnny asking Mommy and Daddy if the people in the next room were sick because of all the moaning.

As morning rolled around, I wandered into the kitchen for a bowl of cereal and a cup of coffee. Passing by the office, I noticed yet another car parked outside our working girl's room. It was a Cadillac Coupe de Ville, gold, with a white vinyl roof and wide whitewall tires. Curb feelers jutted out from the fenders right behind each tire.

"Kinda early to be turning tricks," I said to Mom.

"Yeah, this doesn't look good," she anxiously said.

The hooker's new boyfriend was wearing a bright red derby cap, velvet green jacket with oversized lapels, white bell-bottom pants and patent leather shoes.

"Uh-oh."

"Uh-oh is right," Mom mumbled. "It's her pimp."

"Shit, should we…"

"Call the police? Not yet. Let's see what happens."

Their conversation was getting animated with hands flailing back and forth.

"Guess she's not producing enough or maybe skimming a little off the top before paying her pimp," I suggested.

"Ya, maybe," Mom replied staring at the arguing couple.

The conversation between the hooker and the pimp escalated into a full-on shouting match. About that time, Dad started walking straight toward them.

"What the hell is he doing?" I exclaimed. "That guy probably has a piece in his belt or under the front seat of the Caddy." *Jesus, Dad, this isn't some high school bully. It's a pimp and his prostitute!* "Mom, this is a bad idea. We need to call the cops."

"Okay, get the switchboard ready," she said, while keeping her eyes fixed on Dad and the pimp.

I hastily slapped the headset on and shoved in the jack. The outside line buzzed loudly in my ear.

"Ready."

Dad wore his Clint Eastwood face. We could hear them through the open night window.

"Knock it da hell off, or I'll call the cops," Dad barked. "I don't care vhat you do inside the room, but don't bring your shit outside. You're disturbing our guests. Cool it or get out!" he commanded, getting right up in the pimp's face.

While a violent scumbag, the pimp was smart enough to not cause a scene. There weren't many places left in town that would tolerate prostitution. Get run out of here and he'd have to relocate to Micanopy or Waldo. Not much business in those markets. The pimp backed away, got in his Caddy and left. Our working girl returned to her room.

"Whew, that was close," I said while pulling the jack from the switchboard.

"Yeah, but I don't think we've seen the last of him," Mom said.

"Great and I have the night shift—again!"

# 23

# HELGI

One of our regulars was a professor at UF. Every Tuesday, Dr. Casey Lockwood rented number 15, a single out by the road, to write. At least, that was what he told Mom. Lockwood taught English composition and creative writing. He never stayed overnight. Sporting a ponytail, medium build with a paunch belly, he came across as both arrogant and impish. He probably hung out with fellow intellectuals at UF, whining about having to teach spoiled brats, instead of writing the great American novel.

Maybe he'd be famous one day. We could put something on the sign like "Casey Lockwood wrote here."

My gut told me it was weird that one of my profs rented a room once a week. But nothing qualified as weird at the Florida Motel, not prostitutes, pimps or professors.

One day, a yellow MG Midget pulled in and parked next to Lockwood's car. Out popped a cute little coed.

Blond hair, skin-tight shorts, and a tube top barely holding in her huge ta-tas.

*Holy crap! She's in my comp class. Can't forget a pair like that.*

She had a squeaky voice and was so dumb a box of rocks would have been insulted by the comparison. Dr. Lockwood opened the door before she even knocked.

Writing my ass. Her GPA is about to go up, among other things.

I had more respect for our working girl. At least she was doing an honest, albeit illegal, day's work to turn a buck. Lockwood was getting for free what he should have been paying to our resident hooker. He was taking money out of the economy.

The coed was using her assets to get ahead. She was destroying the grading curve for the entire class. The Professor may have been writing every Tuesday, but *this* Tuesday he was holding "office hours" at The Florida Motel.

An hour later, the coed bounded out of Lockwood's room, hopped into the MG and motored down the road, convertible top down, her blond hair whipping in the wind.

Both were oblivious to the pool boy watching their escapades.

I wasn't sure if this would be awkward or piss me off the next time, I was in comp class. That assumed either of them knew I even existed and connected me to the motel. Doubtful in a freshman class hall with a couple hundred students.

# 24

# HELGI

The next morning as I settled into a seat in comp class and pulled out my notebook, I noticed Office Hours Coed sitting in the front row. Professor Lockwood entered the hall and proceeded down the aisle that divided the rows of tables. Watching him move through the room, my eyes caught another familiar face on the far side of the room. Commuter Girl. I'd been searching for her in every nook and cranny of campus, and she'd been right there in English Comp all along. I was in the same class as Commuter Girl, Professor Fifteen and Office Hours Coed.

*This should be interesting.*

As Dr. Lockwood began his lecture, two hundred sets of eyes focused on the front of the hall. Chairs noisily scooched up to the tables, pre-class chatter fell silent as pens and pencils stood at attention, ready to take down every morsel of test-worthy commentary the prof would spew forth. Office Hours Coed fawned over his every word as if she were in the presence of Thoreau or

Hemmingway. The esteemed professor did his best to look past her to the entire class, attempting to ignore her huge boobs and batting eyes. I thought he did remarkably well, except for a noticeable bulge in his pants.

I didn't feel awkward or angry. In fact, it kinda hit my testosterone-filled funny bone. "Bone,'" what a great word…bone, boner, boning, getting boned. To bone or not to bone. That is the question. Hey, I was in English comp. What did you expect?

Maybe this situation would come in handy down the road. But then, blackmail might cost the motel a regular customer. I decided to keep my identity in my back pocket for now.

As class dismissed, the rush to the exits caused a human traffic jam. Gathering near the end of the line, Commuter Girl got squeezed in my direction. The line inched toward the exit.

*This is my chance. Don't be a douchebag again. Say something!*

Stepping into the aisle as she approached, I swallowed hard and said "Hey, didn't know you were in this class."

"Oh, hi. Yeah, even engineering majors are required to take some undergrad English. It's not really my thing. Why use twenty words to say something when half that will do?"

"Well, I guess if that were the case, we wouldn't have novels," I answered. "What would we do with all those unemployed writers?"

"Good point, but not my problem. I'm only interested in building the roads and bridges that help them get to work. This creative writing stuff drives me crazy," she said, brushing her hair back over her shoulder.

I shrugged. "Comes naturally for me, unlike calculus. I could help you with it," I said. "How about I help you with comp, and you help me with calc. Deal?"

"Deal," she replied with a smile.

"Making deals is what we business majors do. I have a break between classes. Thought I'd head over to the library. You have some time now?"

"Sure, let's go."

"Great. *Carpe diem!*" I quipped.

"You see, right there. I would never think to say *Carpe diem*. Now that's creative," she said.

"I'm Helgi. What's your name?"

"Kristina. Kristina Schmidt," she offered.

"My last name is Moe. What kind of name is Schmidt?"

"German."

"Ah, a German engineer. Makes sense."

"Yeah, kind of a cliché, right?"

"Hey, you said cliché, and you say you don't get this creative writing stuff."

"Ha-ha, what's a Moe?"

"It's Finnish."

The small talk flowed as we walked down the tree-lined sidewalk that ran through the Plaza of the Americas connecting General Purpose Building A to Library North. I opened the large wooden door for her as my mother taught me a gentleman should. She didn't mind. I should've been freaking out or too nervous to speak, but somehow being with her put me at ease. Don't get me wrong. I was thrilled to know her name. We were so close I could've reached out and touched her hand. I didn't. Not yet anyway.

"There's an open table in the back of the room." I said pointing across the cavernous open hall.

Small groups of students worked on assignments together, their muffled conversations rose and faded as we passed. Arriving at the last empty table, we pulled out a couple of chairs at one end, plopped down our backpacks and sat next to each other. Finally, I could look at her for more than a glance. She was even more beautiful up close. Her face held a warm expression. The light reflected off her hair in a way that made her look angelic. She was indeed an angel. My angel. I couldn't help but wonder if Kristina was sent to me for a reason. Was she here to rescue me from the insanity of the Florida Motel? Could she help me find the normalcy I so desperately wanted? *This is nothing more than boy, girl, hormones* I told myself not wanting to get my hopes up.

"So, where are you from?" I asked.

"Gainesville."

"Really? Me too. Where did you go to high school?"

"Buchholz," she said.

"You must live up north. Sorry, but I went to GHS."

"That's okay. I wasn't that into all the high school stuff. Didn't go to any of the football or basketball games. Instead, I was in Mu Alpha Theta, so that made me a geek."

"Mu Alpha whata?" I asked.

"Theta. It's a math club that helps with scholarships."

"So, you have a scholarship?"

"Yes, but it's small. I had to get a student loan, and I have a part-time job. How about you?"

"My parents are paying for my books and tuition. I live at home and work for them."

"You work for your parents?" she asked.

"Yeah, we own a motel. I clean the pool, mow the grass, and run the front desk nights and weekends."

I wasn't ready to tell her about being a maid and doing the laundry. She might think that was strange, because it *was* strange.

"That's sounds so cool. I live at home with my parents. They have regular jobs, mow the lawn on the weekends and we go to church. Pretty boring stuff, but my dad does let me help change the oil in the cars, which is fun."

*Oh my God, she likes to change the oil on cars! Is it too soon to drop the L bomb? Don't want to scare her off. Wait a minute. She thinks the motel is "cool"? I must be in another time dimension.*

"Tell me more about your motel. Where is it? What's it called?" she asked.

"It's the Florida Motel. We're on SW 13$^{th}$ Street before you get to Paynes Prairie."

"You mean the one with the big blue neon sign that looks like Florida?"

"That's the one," I said.

"I love that sign."

"You're welcome to stop by anytime to see it up close. We also have a pool with a slide."

*You idiot—a slide? That's what pops into your head? She's not in elementary school.*

"That sounds like fun," she responded without missing a beat. "Maybe on a weekend when I'm not working."

"That would be great. So, where do you work?"

"At Shands. I got a job as a student assistant."

"What do you do there?"

"File stuff, type letters and answer the phone. Pretty easy and because it's through student services, they work around my class schedule. It helps with my tuition."

"Sounds normal. Wish I could get a job like that, but I've gotta help my folks with the motel."

"Should we get started on your calculus?" she asked.

"Sure. May as well rip off the Band-Aid." I didn't want to do calc because she would see how stupid I was.

"What's that mean?" she asked.

"I mean, I don't get it…calc. It's like I have a mental block of some sort. You really want to help me with it? You're in engineering. You're so far ahead of me," I said opening my text.

"I feel the same way about English comp. People like me write letters on Post-it notes. Let's make another deal. You don't kid me about my mental block with comp, and I won't kid you about calculus. Deal?"

"Deal."

Our mutual tutoring session went on for over an hour, but it felt like only a few precious minutes. I tried to pay attention but was mesmerized by her soft eyes and small, but supple lips. Her enchanting voice soaked through my skin and penetrated my heart. Sine and cosine never sounded so good.

"I've got to go," she said reluctantly. I have class across campus in the engineering building."

"Would you mind if I walked with you? I've got to get back to the motel.

"Okay, but you'll miss the bus, and it's a long walk from engineering to the commuter lot."

"I don't mind. Besides, it's all downhill from there." I

would have walked miles in the wrong direction to be with her a few more minutes.

She cocked her head sideways and nodded toward the door, as if to say 'yes' and was happy I'd asked.

We gathered up our books and stuffed them into our backpacks. Kristina put hers on with both straps over her shoulders. The weight of her books pulled the straps backward which in turn tightened her blouse across her chest making her breasts protrude seductively. They were round, firm and proportional to her size. Unlike the campus coeds, she wore a bra. No nipple fest here. Curiously, I wasn't disappointed. In fact, I found her decorum both arousing and comforting. She wasn't "some floozy" as Grandma would say. This girl was special.

We exited the library and headed across the Plaza to Stadium Drive. Our pace was more like a Sunday stroll than an urgent dash to class. The sleeve of her silk blouse brushed over my arm, sending chills of excitement down my spine. A slight breeze, cooled by the shade of the old oaks, wafted over our faces and gently lifted Kristina's hair from her shoulders. It was fresh, like our relationship.

We resembled a couple of puppies sticking their noses out a car window. With simple joy plastered on our faces, we made our way across campus. We didn't talk much on the way, but volumes were spoken between us.

Arriving at the entrance of the engineering building, my backpack hung over one shoulder, I turned to say goodbye. The motion caused my free hand to circle around and gently collide into hers. She caught it and hooked her pinky finger around mine. She didn't let go. Her touch ran through me like a thousand volts of electricity. It took my breath away. Looking at her, I was lost for words. My throat tightened and mouth went cotton dry. My heart pounded so hard and loud; I was certain she could hear it. Then a mysterious force took over. Gently pulling her toward me, I leaned forward. We kissed. A simple, soft, eyes-closed kiss. My fate with Kristina was sealed. I was officially off the market—not that any of the thousands of girls on campus were even aware of my existence. But if they had been, they would have been cast aside by the earthquake emanating from every fiber of my body. The kiss ended. We didn't speak. Staring into each other's eyes, a million words couldn't have expressed what passed between us that moment. Our faces only inches apart, I felt Kristina's breath on my mouth and inhaled her essence deep into my lungs—and my heart.

Lost in our mutual gaze, a noisy group of students passed, breaking the moment. Kristina nodded in the direction of the engineering building then said apologetically, "I need to go."

"Yes…well…thanks for helping me with calc," I stammered. Not sure I learned anything about calculus, but hopefully there would be more tutoring sessions.

"Thanks for helping me with comp," she said, her eyes continued their hold on me "See you in class?"

"Yes," I whispered.

"Okay. Bye."

"Bye."

Not breaking eye contact, she slowly backed away to go to class. Pinky's still interlocked; our hands rose up from our sides until the widening gap broke the connection. She walked towards the entrance of the building.

Turning to walk away, I glanced back at her one more time. As she opened the door, Kristina tipped her head in my direction, smiled and went inside.

If I'd known what was about to happen, I would never have left her side that day.

# 25

## KRISTINA

After class, Kristina floated back to the commuter lot. She didn't remember a thing the professor said and hadn't taken a single note. Kristina awoke from her love-stricken daze by the sounds of moving chairs as her fellow engineering students got up to leave. The two-hour lecture had passed in an instant.

It was a balmy day, not too hot or humid, but she felt unusually warm. The more she dwelled on Helgi and their walk across campus, the warmer she became. As she got in her car the image of their hands touching and then the kiss—*oh that wonderful, incredible kiss*—replayed through her head. A sensation from deep inside her body caused her heart to pound. Unfamiliar, but pleasant, the tingling stirred deep within her body and settled between her legs.

On the drive home, she couldn't stop thinking about Helgi, his kiss and the pleasing way her body responded.

*When will I see him again?*

# 26

## HELGI

With a spring in my step, I headed out to find Hester. Somehow the motel didn't seem so irritating. Kristina had rocked my world. So much so I almost walked right by the laundry room door. Hester had started her day, and I wanted to pick her brain. I could talk to her about girls. A topic I couldn't broach with Mom and was embarrassed to talk about women with Dad. Besides he probably thought I had figured it out already. He was more concerned with putting food on the table and paying the bills. My love life wasn't on his radar.

But Hester was different. Not my parent and too much older to be my friend. Instead, she acted as mentor and coach, and she wasn't shy about sharing her opinions. Maybe she enjoyed having someone to talk to or she got a kick out of knowing more about something than the little white college boy. In any event, like Grandma, Hester never had anything mean to say, and she always welcomed my questions.

I put a load of sheets in the washer, grabbed a pile of clean towels and walked to the room she was cleaning.

"Morning, Hester," I announced from the side of the cart outside room eight, a single with one queen bed.

"Mornin, baby." She bounced back from inside.

"I brought you some extra towels for the cart."

"Thanks."

"Hey, can I ask you a question?"

"Sure, can you empty this trash for me?"

Before I had a chance to answer, she held the can out the room door and dropped it as she moved by. I instinctively reached out and caught it midflight. Hester was in her cleaning groove. Gliding around the room, her inner music orchestrated every move in perfect sequence. I had unwittingly become her dance partner. Make no mistake, she was leading, and if I wanted to talk about girls, I would have to follow. I emptied the trashcan and brought it back in time for her to whisk it out of my hands and place it in the far corner of the room.

"What's up, baby?"

"Well, um…"

"Don't be shy. Out with it and hands me the bedcover."

I picked up the paisley cover from where she had carefully draped it over a chair and held it out to her. Hester hooked it with a one-armed move, turned on her axis and tossed it over the bed using her classic flying sheets move.

"Well… there's this girl."

"A girl you say?"

"Yeah, I met her on campus. She's a local."

"You likes this girl?" she asked with interest, but not breaking the movement of her cleaning waltz.

"Oh man, Hester. She's beautiful, smart and there's something special about her. She's different than all the other coeds."

"Sos, what you want to know, baby?"

"Baby" was right. I was an infant when it came to girls, dating and relationships. I didn't want to blow it with Kristina. Hester had been down this road before, sometimes with bad endings, which I wanted to avoid at all costs.

"I can't stop thinking about her. I've never felt this way about anyone, and I don't know what to do."

"What you means by, 'what to do?'" she asked while piloting the bedspread over the mattress.

By now I was on the other side of the bed pulling it tight and putting the "tucky'" on the pillows as Hester moved into the bathroom. Toilet brush in hand, she commenced swishing it around the bowl like the conductor of the Boston Pops.

"I don't want to mess this up. How fast should I go? What should I say or do next? We've studied together at the library, and she let me walk her to class. I'm afraid I'm not good enough for her. She's really smart." I blurted out everything.

"Listen to me, baby. You be smart too, and nice. Maybe too nice."

"*Too* nice? What do you mean?"

"Baby, if this girl is as pretty n smart as you be sayin, someone is goin to move in and swoop her up while you be worryin if you be good enough. You gots to take some nichtive, boy. You gots to tell her hows you feel."

"Yeah, but what if I come on too strong? I mean, I want to marry her and make babies."

"Don't be going there yet. Saves the baby makin for later. Girls do like a man who knows what he wants. Someone who looks her in the eyes and tells her she's beautiful 'n' that he wants to be with her and no one else. She wants to be wooed, baby, so don't be grabbin' her booty or stickin' yaw tongue in her mouth."

"Hester!"

"No, I means it, baby. Be nice and gentle-like but makes sure she knows how you feels bout her.

"But what do I say?"

"Don't you be worryin' bout what to say. You a nice boy. Iffen I wasn't so old and already had babies, I'd..."

"You're not old, Hester."

"Thanks, baby." She said with a blushing smile. "Can you get me some soaps from the cart?"

"Sure."

I grabbed the soaps and brought them to the bathroom as she finished wiping out the sink. Swapping her the soaps for the damp towel, I headed back to the cart.

"Thanks, Hester. You need anything from the laundry room?"

"Nope. I's got enough for the checkouts. Now you go get that girl. You hears me?"

"Will do."

As I turned to leave, she had begun vacuuming the shag. This was the last dance for this room, but now she had a new partner...Kirby.

Hester had given me the advice I wanted, and the kick in the butt I needed. I was excited and a little nervous. I didn't have the same confidence that she had in me. Still, I had to do something. Hester was right. I had watched from the sidelines too many times, fretting about what to say to girls, only to watch other guys move in and swoop them away. There was too much raging testosterone on campus to leave Commuter Girl to chance.

# 27

## HELGI

One motel thing led to another and before I knew it, Mom was clearing the dinner table, Dad was on the couch watching Walter Cronkite and I had settled in at the front desk for the evening shift. Traffic on the road slowed considerably at night. Passing cars were silhouettes in the setting sun. A few guests sat outside their rooms enjoying the evening breeze.

Expecting a sleepy summer night, I planned to get in some solid study time—if I could keep my mind off Kristina. Once all patrons were safely in their rooms, I could see their lights still on through the separation of the curtains. One by one, they went out. The neon-lit VACANCY announced we were open. A balmy breeze soothed the motel to sleep.

Outside, near the back corner the office, there was an opening along the walkway that allowed us to pass through from the back of the property. The private driveway in the rear led to a small paved road. To the left was 13th street or "the road," fronting the motel. To the right was a sparsely populated residential area. Unlike the front of the motel, everything out back was pitch-black at night. Only a sliver of light from the kitchen window spilled out to the garage port before abruptly falling well short of the tree line along the back of the property. Once the sun went down, the end of the gravel driveway disappeared out of sight. No one could be seen coming or going after dark. Further, the corner just inside the rear access was not visible from the office.

Our quiet evening was about to explode.

I looked up every so often to give my eyes a study break and glance over the parking lot to the entrance, checking the property. If a car turned in, their headlights were impossible to ignore and gave me a few seconds to shift gears from studying-student to clerk.

At 11p.m. the office door shook with a bang, jolting me from my textbook. The force rattled all the glass in the room.

"What the hell!" I said out loud.

A large, black guy stood outside the door. Surprised the door was locked, he jumped back looked around to see if anyone was around. I was glad for our motel safety rule: when the sun goes down, the door gets locked.

"Lemme in. I needs a room," he said unconvincingly.

"Come around here," I said while pointing to the night window.

At the same time Dad, who was in the kitchen munching a bedtime snack, peaked out the dining-room window. What he saw scared the crap out of him. Crouching in the dark corner behind the night window was another man. Short, with a heavy build and a ball cap covering his head, he held a sawed-off shotgun. Dad knew what was happening. Clearly, their plan was to have the first guy (the doorman) enter the office to distract the night clerk (me!) and then have the second man enter to hold up the place.

"Don't open the door. It's a robbery," Dad said sternly, but quietly, not to spook the guy with the shotgun. It sounded like a whisper shout.

"You need to come over to the window," I repeated.

Heart pounding in my chest, I didn't know what to do. Call the police or run inside the living quarters to hide. Dad stationed Mom in the dining room to keep an eye on Shotgun Guy and then came out to the office.

"We're closed. No rooms available," he barked from behind the desk.

*Christ, I hope they're illiterate. The VACANCY sign is still on.*

Doorman moved around to the teller window. The Old Man had his .38 Special, which we kept below the counter. He was between me and the bad guys. I slowly retreated to the switchboard.

"Don't calls the cops," Doorman ordered, pulling a handgun from his back. He stuck it through the narrow open slot of the night window. Dad immediately slammed it down on his wrist causing the gun to point up to the ceiling.

"Ow. Shit!" he yelled, wincing in pain.

Doorman's knees buckled as he tried to pull his hand out. Mom was so close to Shotgun Guy, she could have reached through the jalousie window and grabbed him by the collar. She screamed. Startled and still crouched, Shotgun Guy pulled the trigger. The shot, grazed Doorman right in the ass. The impact caused him to fire his pistol. The bullet exploded through the office and out the far side, hurling shards of glass everywhere. Ducking, Dad fell backward, hitting the corner of the desk. Arms flailing, he squeezed off a round of the .38 striking the fluorescent lights in the ceiling, which brought down the entire fixture. Hanging from the wiring it swung down and cracked Dad in the head, knocking him to the floor. He crashed into the counter, scattering the neatly stacked little soaps. Mom continued screaming from the dining room.

"Yeow!" Doorman screeched at Shotgun Guy. "Yo' shot me motherfuckah!"

"Oh man, you bleedin' real bad. Yo' ass is half blown off!"

"No shit, asshole. Help me get my hand outta this damn window. It's stuck."

Shotgun Guy stood up to help. Sweating profusely, he yanked him hard, wrenching his hand through the slim opening. Doorman dropped his pistol inside the office as it wouldn't fit through the narrow slot.

"Ouch, you ripped the skin off my hand!"

"Shut the fuck up. We gotta get outta here 'fore the cops show up."

Making their escape the same way they came in, Doorman put one arm over the Shotgun Guy's shoulders while clasping his ass with his freehand. They hobbled down the hidden walkway, through the back entrance, and disappeared into the dark abyss behind the motel.

I stood frozen in place. Dad was lying on the floor, covered in little soaps. The light swung back and forth over the desk as acrid gun smoke burned my nostrils. Shattered glass was everywhere. Lights went on in the guest rooms, but no one came out. Mom ran into the office.

"Call the police! Oh God, Sven you okay? Did you get hit?"

"Ya, I'm ok, Leena. Sonofabitch shot out da vindow. Dat's going to cost us."

"Vindow! Dey tried to shoot you, and all you can dink of is da vindow?" she said incredulously while cradling his head.

The stress caused them both to relapse to their native Finn accents.

As I turned to call the police, I saw Fogman standing in front of the shattered window brandishing his BFK.

"Dude, you guys okay?" he said in a coherent voice.

Surprised, I hesitated to respond.

"Is anyone hurt in there?"

"Ah…I think my dad hit his head, but no one got shot," I answered in disbelief. I was having a lucid conversation with Number Nine.

"Call the police. I'll stand guard out here." He said taking up a defensive position by the door.

*What the hell is going on? Am I in an episode of the Twilight Zone?*

"9-1-1, what's your emergency?"

"Ra…ra…rhaa" I stammered. Up until now it was like watching a TV show in slow motion. It wasn't until the 9-1-1 operator started talking that I realized this wasn't television and our attackers were not actors. I lost it.

"Sir, what is your emergency?"

"Ra…ROBBERY!" I shouted into the headset. Two

men tried to rob us. They had guns. I think one of them got shot."

"Is anyone there hurt?

"My dad fell when the light hit him in the head."

"Did he get shot?"

"No, he landed on the little soaps."

"He slipped on soap?"

"No, you dope, he didn't slip on soap. They got knocked off the desk when he fell after the light hit him in the head."

"Settle down, sir. No need for name calling. I'm trying to help."

"Sorry, ma-am."

"That's okay. The police are on their way. Did you say someone got shot?"

"I think so. There were two guys. One hid behind the night window. When Leena—"

"You mean your mother, sir?"

"Yes, how'd you know—?"

"That Leena is your mother? This *is* the Florida Motel, correct?"

"Yes?"

"The same motel that called in a naked lady report."

"Yes?"

"I was on duty that night, sir," she said as if annoyed.

*You've got to be fucking kidding me. Two guys just tried to rob us at gunpoint and blew out the office window. One bad guy shot the other bad guy's ass off, and I'm feeling embarrassed by the 9-1-1 operator because we keep calling with crazy shit!*

Thankfully, before I spoke my mind, I heard the sirens of the cop cars approaching.

"The police are here, ma'am."

"Okay, Florida Motel. The officers will take over from here…again."

I pulled the plug before I said something that would get me in trouble. Two police cars screeched to a stop in front of the office. The officers jumped out, drew their guns and pointed them at Fogman. "Drop the weapon!" they ordered.

Fogman immediately dropped the knife. It pierced the blacktop still warm and soft from the sun, landing straight up.

"Get on the ground and put your hands behind you back."

Again, Fogman complied without a word. Seemed as if he'd been through this routine before.

As the police approached to cuff him, I shouted through the broken glass, "Officers, he's not the robber. He's one of our guests."

"Stay in the office, sir."

After the police got everything under control, they began to sort out the details. A few minutes later, they uncuffed Fogman. "Sorry for the misunderstanding, sir."

"No problem, officers. You were only doing your job." Fogman replied. "I was an MP back in Nam. That's the bayonet from my M1."

"Really, when were you there?" One officer asked.

"Sixty-five to sixty-nine."

"Sixty-eight to seventy-two for me," the officer replied. "That was some nasty shit."

"It was a total shit sandwich," Fogman replied.

While the two of them shared war stories, the other officer called for an ambulance and put out an all-points bulletin for the perps.

"They won't get too far," he said. "If one of them did get hit by a shotgun, he's going to end up in the emergency room or bleed to death. Don't worry, we'll find them."

An ambulance pulled in, and the EMTs checked out Dad. He had a pretty bad gash on his forehead from the flying fluorescents.

"We need to take you to the hospital. Make sure everything's ok. You've sustained a bad hit to your head," said one of them to Dad while looking at Mom.

"No go hospital. Mus…clean da office," Dad slurred. He was confused.

"Sven…ah…da vindow…I don't…" Mom stammered incoherently. Everything had hit her at the same time. Confused, scared and worried about Sven, she didn't to know what to do. At that moment, wearing a furry, pink bathrobe and hairnet, Grandma scurried out of her bedroom and into the office, while putting in her teeth. I had no idea she could move that fast. Suddenly, something switched on inside me and I took control of the situation.

"Dad, you're going to the hospital. Mom, you go with him in the ambulance. He might need an x-ray or something. Grandma, you watch the office. I'll clean up the glass and board up the window," I said with authority. A profound sense of responsibility for my parents and the motel bolstered by adrenalin pumping through my veins took over.

"We'll keep a unit here and patrol the area the rest of the night," the Vietnam-vet officer added.

"And I'll take up a position outside my room. We've

got your back, dude," Fogman said with a renewed sense of purpose in his voice.

The EMT spoke to Dad, "Sir, we really need to get you to the hospital,"

"You're going, Sven, and dats dat," Mom ordered.

They loaded him into the ambulance. Mom sat in the jump seat beside him. While one of the EMTs tended to Dad's injuries, the other shut the heavy metal doors. As the ambulance pulled away, its red lights pulsating off the motel's walls, I'd undergone a change. My boyhood died that night. They had assaulted our family and damaged our little motel. It was one thing for me to complain about it, but no one, and I mean no one, had the right to attack us. Anger replaced fear, followed by a sense of commitment and loyalty to the Florida Motel.

# 28

# HELGI

Dad was hurt worse than we thought. Not only did he have a concussion, the doctors also found a blood clot in his leg that had nothing to do with the robbery. They said it could clear up with medicine and rest after a few weeks or it could take months, but there was a significant risk of it breaking loose and going to his heart. I would need to help run the motel full time until he recovered. My academic fate was sealed until Dad got back on his feet.

"What will you do about your classes, Helgi?" Mom asked.

"Don't worry, Ma. They will let me drop my classes for the semester. We don't get the tuition back, but it won't hurt my grades. I'll take them over again when Dad is better."

"I'm sorry, Helgi."

"Don't worry, Mom. Hopefully, it will only be one semester. I can take a couple of heavy loads to make up the time when I go back. Everything will be okay. I'm not sure "it's good that this happened" as grandma would say, but I need to be here for now," I said.

Mom broke down in tears.

While Dad convalesced with Monty Hall in the living room, Grandma manned the front desk and Hester cleaned rooms.

"I'm running up to campus to drop my classes. Be right back."

"Okay, take your time." Mom sighed.

That was a strange thing for her to say. She must have felt bad that I had to quit school to help them. For all her specious nonsupport, she wanted me to get a college degree. They both did.

My mind numbed on the way to campus. I passed Graffiti Wall without a glance. Coeds didn't catch my eyes. Dropping my classes wasn't bothering me as much as the thought of not seeing Kristina. I didn't have her number. Didn't know how to find her. Couldn't explain why I wouldn't be there anymore. I drove by Museum Road.

*No DWC today, no commuter lot or commuter bus, no classes or library, no…Kristina!*

Sadness coursed through my body. Pain seared my gut. My eyes welled up. I wasn't mad at Mom and Dad or even the motel. I knew what I needed to do, but I also felt horrible. Kristina had worked her way into my heart and soul. The warm glances, easy talk and the single, most precious touch of our hands the day I walked her to class, told me I had met the one…the only one for me. Somehow, someday we'd meet again. I prayed she didn't meet someone else in the meantime. If she had half the feelings for me as I did for her, we'd find each other again. Or was it all wishful thinking?

*That kiss. Was it our first or last?*

As I parked in front of the Bursars Office, my emotions caught up with me. I sat there, broke down and sobbed. Finally, getting a grip, I wiped the tears on the sleeves of my Gator t-shirt, got out of the car and trudged up the stairs to the Bursars Office. Minutes later, it was done. Classes dropped, I got in my little blue Road Runner as a nonstudent. Nothing more than another local heading to work. The campus disappeared into my rearview mirror and out of my life as I headed back to the Florida Motel.

# 29

# HELGI

The city bus route ended a mile past the motel with a stop near our entrance. Good thing for Hester, as she didn't have a car. Without the bus, she couldn't have worked for us or any other motel along the road. She'd have been limited to the graveyard shift at the Seven Eleven next to her place in the hood. That would've been tough as a single mom. There was no daddy around, and, even if there was, I don't think Hester would have let him near her babies. She wanted better for them and to set a good example by working for a living.

Walking down the parking lot from the bus stop, Hester's expression shifted from her usual upbeat self to one of concern when she saw the boarded-up office window.

"What happened?" she asked.

Funny how stress changes people's dialects. Mom and Dad revert to Finnish and Hester speaks perfect English.

"Two guys tried to rob us." I replied.

"Ms. Leena okay?"

"Yes, but Dad was hurt."

"Bad?"

"No, but he can't work for a while."

"What went down?" she asked.

I told her the whole story. She smirked and chuckled at Doorman getting shot in the ass by his buddy. Her chuckling stopped when the seriousness of what happed…what almost happened to us sunk in. We treated Hester with respect, spoke to her as an equal and included her in our lives. We were like family to her and those two punks had threatened it.

"I tears em up iffen I finds em," she exclaimed while smacking a clenched fist into the other hand. Hester had a strong defensive attitude as a condition of survival in the ghetto.

"Won't be too hard. One of them is a real half-ass." I said trying to ease her fears.

She smiled.

"Here's the list of checkouts and stay overs. You should have enough towels and sheets to get started. It's been a little crazy around here. Didn't have time to start the laundry yet. Once Mom is done tending to Dad, she'll take over the front desk, and I'll get it going."

"I's get the wash going before I starts cleanin', Mr. Helgi."

Hmm, *Mr.* Helgi. That was different. Wasn't sure I liked the sound of it. She must have sensed a change in me that morning. Did this mean no more "baby?"

"Thanks, Hester," I said, moving on to the next thing on my to-do list.

I knew her normal routine would help take her mind

off the attempted robbery. We needed Hester to be herself.

The window repairman pulled in as she headed out for the day's work. The plywood covering the broken glass screamed to all our guests that something bad had happened. Stay overs checked out a day early. Cars pulling in from the road slowed then abruptly left. More than an eyesore, it cost us business. We put on our happy faces like makeup concealing a scar. Unfortunately, this wound would never fully heal. Our motel life had been crazy, colorful and unpredictable, but in a good, if not a fun way. No matter what came at us, there was a sense of adventure to the biz. We lived in our own little theme park with wild rides and funny characters that kept us on our toes and entertained. Life before may not have been normal for anyone else in the world, but it was our "normal." The intrusion upended our lives like a rollercoaster coming off its tracks. Wild and crazy quickly became scary. Eventually, the families, hospital people, Gators fans and even our Number nines brought back a semblance of normalcy. The robbery had dimmed the lights of our park, but it couldn't turn them off.

The old motel was growing on me. My sense of duty quelled my desire to leave. The motel's ledgers replaced textbooks. Campus had become a distant memory—classes faded away. It was as if I'd never been there, except for Commuter Girl. Kristina's image popped into my head anywhere and at any time. Front desk, laundry room, cleaning the pool, it didn't matter. There she was, clear as the day I first saw her on the bus. The memory of that first touch of our hands still sent jolts of electricity through my entire body. Our kiss haunted me.

The motel biz is 24/7. With Dad out of commission, there was no spare time to get away. Wandering about campus to find Kristina was out of the question. Where was she today? Was she looking for me? Could she ever forgive me?

# 30

# HELGI

Summer yielded to fall, and the sweltering heat had abated in Gainesville. Campus bustled with the semester in full swing. The student body was highest at this time as freshman had yet to face their college midterms. The first crop of dropouts would be harvested by the end of the term. Florida was a tough to get in and tougher to get through.

Fall also brought football season and UF was a football school. Sure, we had the full complement of other sports, but they all paled in comparison to SEC Football. On home game weekends, Gainesville's population practically doubled. Alumni came from all over the state, and even from Georgia and Alabama, to cheer on the mighty Gators. We had the coolest mascot. There are more popular, recognizable college mascots, but none cooler than a gator. Your mascot may be cute, but ours will chomp yours to pieces.

There was a buzz of energy on campus and around

town with the return of football season. You'd have to be brain dead not to get caught up in the spirit. Everyone in Gainesville were Gators regardless of being students and alumni. With Florida football ingrained in the culture, there was no bigger event than homecoming weekend.

## 31

## CHIP

Chip Cantwell was nothing more than another smug little frat boy with GQ looks and a wallet full of Daddy's money. He even drove a brand-new Fiat Spyder, Ferrari red with tan leather seats. What a cliché! He could have had any girl on campus he wanted, especially the box-of rocks coeds from sorority row. Most of them were only there to get their MRS degree.

The Chipster was smart, conniving and focused on one thing only…hooking up with a local chick. He had a bet with his frat brothers to see who could be first to have sex with a local girl. There would be bonus points if she was a virgin.

Grabbing a seat in his engineering class he spotted a plain Jayne student sitting in the front row. She was slender, with long, flowing straight hair. She was clearly by herself, leafing through her notes and not talking to anyone else.

*Looks doable. Sitting alone, drab clothing, No nails. No tits. Must be a local. Turn around now so I can get a look at your face.*

Not that what she looked like mattered. He had joked with his bros that they had to be all in for the bet. No backing out for ugly chicks. No matter if they were a one or two bagger, they had to do them to win. In fact, ugly, fat chicks were the best targets due to their low self-esteem. They'd jump in the sack with anyone let alone a rich frat boy. When she turned to face the professor at the podium, he saw her face. She was pretty. For a nanosecond the Chipster was taken aback by the girl in the front row. She was good looking…in a farmer's daughter way.

But he quickly regained his senses. To him, she was nothing more than a goal to achieve, another notch on his conquest bedpost and all the bragging rights that came with it. This one might be a little more challenging. He'd have to play the game with all his charms and skills. She may be a local, but she's is in engineering, so she's not stupid. Too bad she wasn't a brainless sorority chick. They were as easier than fat chicks.

Chip walked into his frat house with a cocky smirk on his face.

"Dude, you didn't already…" one of his brothers shouted out from the group chugging beers on the over-sized leather couch on the main room.

"No, but I have one marked. You all might as well just pay me know" Chip bellowed.

Boos and hisses thundered from the couch. A red Solo cup full of beer flew past his head. He ducked, grabbed a beer and started chugging while his frat brothers started chanting. Pussy…pussy…pussy!

## 32

## KRISTINA

Kristina arrived early to comp class. She hoped Helgi would be there today. Their last encounter simmered in her heart. She didn't know why he had disappeared. It wasn't like him or at least it wasn't like the image she had painted of him. Hundreds of freshmen strolled into the huge theater-like hall and took their seats. Trying to keep cool, Kristina's heart skipped a beat every time the door opened. The bright Florida sunlight silhouetted the students momentarily hiding their faces until the door closed behind them. This only compounded to her anxiety. Disappointed he didn't show, she started feeling insecure wondering if he regretted what happened the day, he walked her to class.

*Why isn't he here? Was it something I said? Was the kiss too much too fast?*

She wandered aimlessly through the library— even went up to the Stacks. A place her dad had warned her to no go lone as a female student. Helgi's wasn't to be found anywhere. Depressed she made her way across campus to Engineering. Still looking around for Helgi, her feelings of self-doubt turned to anger. Anger at Helgi for disappearing without a word. Anger at herself for having made such a big deal out of a kiss that clearly didn't mean anything to him.

*Stupid, stupid, stupid.*

# 33

## KRISTINA

Not her usual happy self, Kristina quietly worked with her engineering classmates on a group project. She could tell one of the guys in her group, Chip Cantwell, had his eyes on her for some time. "Hey Kristina, Homecoming is in two weeks. My fraternity is building a float for the parade. Would you like to join us?" he asked, flipping his styled blond hair to one side.

"No thanks, I have to go work after class," she responded, attempting to brush him off.

She had wandered campus all semester looking for Helgi. He'd disappeared. She thought they had something. *Guess I was mistaken.* Still, she wanted to see him again, even if he didn't want to see her.

"Aww come on; it'll be fun. And we need your help. You're the smartest one in engineering," Chip cajoled. "It would be like an applied design class. Very useful for job interviews."

Kristina shrugged. "Well, maybe it wouldn't hurt," she said.

"Great, we meet in the evenings and on weekends to work on the float, so it won't interfere with your job."

Kristina was still a young woman whose natural urges and her brief encounter with Helgi had awakened her desires. She liked how it made her feel. She missed it. There was a hole in her heart from Helgi's abrupt disappearance. Maybe this Chip guy could fill it or at least be a distraction from Helgi, she thought.

*Couldn't hurt anything…right?*

As Homecoming weekend approached, Kristina worked on the float with Chip and the rest of the fraternity. They were getting to know each other, and she thought he was nice, maybe even a little cute. "Hey Kristina, there's room to ride on the float. Would you like to join us?" Chip asked with his orthodontically perfect smile.

"I don't know, Chip. I've always watched the parade with my family."

"It'll be a blast. You can wave to them as we go by. Wouldn't that be cool?"

"That does sound like fun, and it would thrill them to see me up there."

"That's my girl," Chip said as he gave her a celebratory hug.

Kristina hugged him back, but it was a little too close and a little too long. Still, she was happy to be a part of the group and riding on a float in the homecoming parade. It was a big deal, especially to a local. Usually, only the frat boys, sorority coeds and the football team got to ride on the floats. Still, there was something about Chip that gave her pause.

*Hmm…he seems perfect. Too perfect?*

She had seen through Helgi's naiveté with girls. She admired it in a way. Helgi was genuine. Little did she know that Chip only wanted to get in her pants. Would she see through his deceitful manipulation or was her vision blurred by the pain of losing Helgi with no explanation?

## 34

## HELGI

Homecoming was a week away. We were back in a groove at the motel and Dad was recovering. We knew he was feeling better because he was up and around enough to complain about things not getting done or not done *correctly*. It looked like my academic sabbatical might only be for one semester.

Casey Lockwood continued holding office hours in number fifteen. Since I was there full time, we ran into each other more often, but he never recognized me from his comp class. I was even on desk duty twice when he checked in. His presence tore open the wounds of losing Kristina. Only Hester understood the pain I felt.

Mom took over the front desk, and I strode to the laundry room, gathered towels and soaps for the cart and crossed the parking lot to where she was cleaning. She didn't need anything, but I needed an excuse to talk to her. Handing her supplies she didn't ask for was getting old, but Hester didn't mind.

"Hey, Hester. Brought you some supplies for the cart."

"Thanks, baby," she replied, knowing why I was there. "When you be goin back to school?"

"Baby" was refreshing to hear again.

"Hopefully, next semester," I said. "Dad seems to be better; don't you think?"

"Mr. Sven be jokin' with me this mornin'. I thinks he be okay. He's a strong man that Mr. Sven."

"Yeah, he and Mom are nipping at each other. He must be recovering."

"You ever go see that little girlfriend of yours?" she asked.

"No, we had to take care of the motel. She probably wouldn't have understood why I couldn't get away from the motel."

"Oh, she be undertandin' alright. Iffen she sparks on you the way you sparks on her."

"You think so, Hester?" A glint of hope sprang forth in my voice.

"I knows so, baby. Now, don't you be waitin' until you goes back to school. You git up there, finds her and tells her how you feel."

"What if I'm too late? What if she's already met someone else? I don't think I could handle seeing her with another guy."

"Lordy, lordy, boys all be the same. You thinks you be in charge. Y'all thinks the man be deciding these things when it's the girls who be in charge. You see lions n' tigers n' such on TV? It's always the females that choose who they mate with, not the boys with their big fancy hair.

Heck, I sees it with mutts outside my crib. It be the bitches that tell those mangy old studs who gets to ridem."

"Hester! Kristina isn't a dog and I'm not trying to jump her bones," I said feigning shock and dismay. Hester had a way of cutting to the chase. Her advice was direct, honest and unedited. If you didn't want to hear what she had to say and how she said it, then don't ask.

"Maybe not you, but someone up there on campus wants to, and you best be strutting your stuff too before she chooses someone else. And don't be thinkin' you're not interested in doing the nasty with Ms. Kristina. I sees the way you look when you talks of her. You be all flush in the face 'n all."

"Hester!" I knew I was blushing.

"You knows I be right. Now, you go finds that girl… Ms. Kristina."

Hester was right…again. Not only did she have her Ph.D. in maid service, she clearly minored in psych or anthropology or both. Why was I paying all this tuition to Florida when I had Professor Hester for free?

Her words motivated me. They also sent a ping of fear through my heart and sent me reeling off into a hormone fueled fantasy. Scenes of some other guy touching Kristina, kissing her soft lips and caressing her played out in my jealous head like some sort of horror movie. The pain made me change the channel.

*I hold her close, passionately kissing her. I slip my tongue into her mouth. She responds with a slight moan while wrapping her tongue around mine. Her breasts…* "Baby, you all right? Hester's voice broke my fantasy-induced trance and jolted me back to reality.

*Crap! Hester's right. I am thinking about Kristina in that way.*

No matter what lofty pedestal I put her on, I was still an eighteen-year-old, testosterone-filled horn dog. This was becoming an all-too-recurrent event. From naked ladies, bikini-clad band chicks and now, erotic fantasies while cleaning rooms with Hester, I needed to get this under control before some guest called the police to report a pervert walking around the motel with a stiffy.

"Uh…what? You say something?" I stammered.

"You seems distracted. What's up?"

"What do you mean 'up'?" I asked, stepping behind the cart to hide my…um…issue. Standing straight up from a semi-crouching position, my "issue" slammed into the side of the steel cart.

I moaned as my forehead scrunched and my eyeballs rolled back into my head. It was a feeble attempt to hide my arousal. Hester grinned at me. She knew what was "up." It was her way of saying, "I told you so," while sparing my dignity.

With that special pain that only guys can relate to radiating up my back, I bent over and hobbled to the privacy of the laundry room. Coach Hester had not only given me another pep talk, she had presented a life lesson on relationships—specifically—the undeniable truth of the birds and the bees. And she did it by using my hormones as the chapter example, complete with a live, in-class cause-and-effect demonstration.

I wanted to go to campus and soon. But I had dropped all my classes and registration for spring semester wasn't open yet. While technically still a student at UF, I didn't have any reason to be there. But, talking with Hester brought Kristina front and center. I had to find her. To explain everything. To tell her I had feelings…no…that's weak…that I loved her.

*The parade! That's it. I'll go to the homecoming parade.*

# 35

## KRISTINA

Kristina had parked her car in the commuter lot when Chip pulled in to pick her up. Even though it was Saturday morning, there wasn't any parking at his frat house. Campus was already buzzing with activity and extra police were on duty to ticket illegally parked cars.

"Good morning, gorgeous," Chip said from his little red Spider. The top was down. "Hop in; we're almost ready to move the float in line for the parade."

"Hi, Chip. Love your car. Gotta love a ragtop, right?"

"It was a high school graduation present from my parents." he said, playing the wealth card to impress her.

She wasn't.

# 36

# HELGI

It was officially home-coming weekend. The parade would take place in the morning followed by the afternoon game. The campus bulged with visiting alumni parking their huge RVs next to Florida Field for some serious tailgating. They were called Bull Gators, and it took a minimum donation of ten grand to the university to secure a coveted parking space. But tailgating wasn't confined to the alumni. Every frat house and dorm was gearing up for an entire day of boozing. The weekend-long cocktail party started the night before with Gator Growl. Originally the pregame pep rally, the Growl had escalated into a huge nighttime show that filled the entire football stadium. Booze flowed like a rain-swelled river, especially in the under-age student section. The otherwise overzealous campus police were conveniently blind once a year for Gator Growl. The whole thing wrapped up with one of the biggest fireworks shows in the state, even bigger than Disney World. Most of the student body stayed up all night. The old

Bull Gators would retreat to their RVs for some shut eye and detox.

Turning into the commuter lot, always the car nut, I noticed a cool little sports car pulling out. When it came to automobiles I didn't discriminate. Model Ts, 50s hotrods, muscle cars or European sports cars, I liked them all.

*Fiat Spider, red with tan interior, body designed by Pininfarina. The same Pininfarina that designs Ferraris. Gotta love a ragtop.*

The Fiat passed by me. All its details ran through my thick head without having paid any attention to the people inside. The parade was about to start, and I needed to find a place along University Avenue to look for Kristina. Walking up through campus, a troubling thought snaked through my brain. I thought I recognized the girl in the passenger seat of the Spider.

*Was that? Nah…couldn't be. Could it?*

The thought of Kristina with someone else gnawed at me. The homecoming parade was a big deal and going alone wasn't normal. If she was there, she would most likely with someone. I only hoped she'd be with some friends.

When I arrived at University Avenue, spectators were already three-deep in front of the stadium, so I moved in the direction of the business school, away from the start of the parade. The route turned at the corner of University and 13th causing a bottle neck which slowed the procession. It was a great spot if you wanted to see the floats a bit longer.

I looked for Kristina. *Might be on the other side with her family or some friends.* Scanning the throngs of people lining the street revealed a fatal flaw in my plan. Everyone wore

Gator garb. It was like campus camouflage. They all looked the same, and the thickening crowd of fans moved about like a sea of orange and blue waves ebbing and flowing down University Avenue. It would be an act of dumb luck to run into Kristina. I'd have a better chance of finding her if I pulled one of those old books from its resting place in the library and sat there and read all day, hoping she would come by to study.

But I decided to stick around and watch the festivities. I hadn't had a break from the motel since the robbery. It was fun being back on campus with all that energy and surrounded by all those carefree students. Ha, "carefree students," I saw them differently now. I felt less like them than ever before, but not in a bad way. They all seemed younger, more immature.

BOOM!

A blast shot forth from a cannon, officially starting the parade way down University past the stadium. The floats, Gator marching band, cheerleaders, Shriner's go-carts and ROTC guys, began flowing out from the intramural fields next to the law school where they had been staged. It would be a while before they reached my spot on the route.

## 37

## KRISTINA

"You ready for this, Krissy?" Chip said. "Here, let me help you." He grabbed her outreached hand and pulled her up on the float. No one had ever called her Krissy. She thought it was odd but was too excited to dwell on it.

"Come on up to the front with me. We can see everything, and everyone can see us. It's the best spot," he said, taking her hand and walking along the side of the float.

As they glided on to the parade route, Kristina beamed with excitement.

*This can't be real. Am I really on a homecoming float?*

The mighty Gator marching band led the way announcing, in grand John Philip Sousa style, the start of the parade. You heard them before students in their bold, blue uniforms and tall fringed hats materialized like the old fife and drum corps advancing in front of the troops. The volume of the drumline shook your bones, and the trumpets made your ears ring.

Then the floats began drifting by, interspersed from

time to time by one of the local high school bands, cheerleaders, and the fire department. They would flex and sway from side to side under the weight of all the students piled on top. On occasion, the parade would come to a stop from the accordion effect rippling down the procession. The sudden braking of the tow vehicle would cause the riders to lurch forward. Chip took the opportunity to put his arms around Kristina's waist to keep her from falling.

"Isn't this awesome?" he asked, holding her close after another stop.

"It's great," she replied, turning outward to free herself from his chivalrous grip.

His advances made her uncomfortable. This was the homecoming parade for crying out loud. Kristina thought public displays of affection were inappropriate. At least that's what the nuns had drilled into her before she went to public school. It's not that she didn't like it. She didn't want to do it in front of everyone—unless it was kissing Helgi in front of the engineering building. More importantly, she didn't have those kinds of feelings for Chip. She really believed this was all about the parade—nothing more. But Kristina worried it wouldn't look that way to anyone who saw them spooning on deck the float. Lost in a gaze, their float passed by a noisy group of students, breaking the awkward moment.

# 38

# HELGI

As a Kappa Kappa Dickhead float drew near the corner of University and 13th, I was fully engaged in the homecoming spirit. Hootin' and hollerin' as they passed by, I wished I had gone to the Gator Growl and kicked myself for not getting a ticket to the game. For the first time in months, I was having fun and feeling like a student again. I was back on campus, yet, it didn't feel like an escape from the motel.

The parade lurched to a stop. There, right before my eyes stood Kristina on the front of the Dickhead float with some tall, good looking, blond-haired, frat boy embracing her from behind. His arms tightly wrapped around her waist held their bodies together. My heart stopped. Pain shot through every nerve in my body… searing, scorching pain.

OH GOD, PLEASE NO screamed through every fiber of my body.

Stunned, I couldn't move. Couldn't run from the sight. Think of the most dreadful, horrible thing you could ever imagine happening to you. Then envision some power preventing you from turning away. Making you stand there, forcing your eyes wide open to look at it. The moment I saw Kristina—my Kristina—held by another man was hell on Earth.

As the parade started to move again, she glanced in my direction, but didn't see me in the sea of orange and blue. The float turned down 13th and disappeared.

I couldn't breathe. Jealousy raged through my blood, overtaken by a tsunami of anguish and grief. Heartbreak crushed my soul. The parade evaporated from my consciousness. My body finally took over, gasping in air from not breathing. Shocked and numb, I stumbled while turning to leave.

A stranger caught me. "Hang on there, buddy. Too much to drink, man?" he said while putting his arm around my shoulder to steady me.

I looked up at him. Lifeless, I could barely move my head. He could tell from my face that booze wasn't the problem.

"Hey man, you want me to get some help. Call the EMTs or something?"

I pursed my lips and shook my head with a quiet "No thanks," steadied myself and staggered away. The walk to the commuter lot felt like an eternity. All I wanted was to get off campus and go home…home to the Florida Motel.

## 39

## KRISTINA

Looking over the crowd as their float shuddered to a stop making the turn on to 13$^{th}$ Street, Kristina sensed something or someone.

*Was that? Nah…couldn't be. Could it?*

Thoughts of Helgi overwhelmed her as Chip once again embraced her from behind. The parade continued to Museum Road where it ended.

Making their way back across campus, she became somber and distant.

"Hey, you okay?" Chip asked.

"Oh yes, I think I'm tired from all the excitement," she replied.

"You're going to the game, right? I have some extra tickets. We have great seats for the fraternity."

"Um, I've got plans with my family," she fibbed.

"Plans for what? It's homecoming. What else would you be doing today?" he asked in a judgmental tone.

"Well, um…" She stammered for words.

Lying didn't come naturally to her, but the homecoming spirit was gone, and she wasn't in the mood for a football game. Thinking about Helgi reignited all her feelings for him. She knew she wanted him back. She didn't care why he had disappeared. She would forgive him. The anger she felt before gave way once again to a flood of self-doubt. Now, Kristina feared it was all her fault. Did she drive him away? Was she too nerdy? Too much of a tomboy? Too prim and proper? She should have told him how she felt.

*I'm such an idiot. All books. No boys. Why can't I be a normal girl?*

# 40

# HELGI

Once at the commuter lot, it became clear I was trapped on campus. The return route of the parade took it through campus on Museum Road, turned up Frat Row and back the intramural fields. The floats were parked along the way in front of their respective fraternities. The Police had also blocked off all other campus roads for traffic control. Still in a state of disbelief, I was in no condition to drive. To pass the time and get hold of myself, I walked over to Lake Alice.

*Maybe Old One Eye will be there.*

Lake Alice was in the southwest corner of campus right along Museum Road. A local attraction because of the alligators that inhabited it. The inspiration for UF's mascot, the lake was filled with hundreds of the toothy reptiles. Gators don't like humans and rarely attack anything bigger than them unless you got too close to their nests. Many locals came down in the evenings to feed them leftovers. They loved chicken.

I shuffled through the dirt parking area and out onto

a small peninsula jutting into the lake. Dozens of gators cruised around with only their eyes and snouts poking out of the water's surface. When they moved, their backs rose out of the water from the force of their powerful tails thrusting them forward.

They were so smart they could tell if you had something for them to eat. If you did, the entire lake came alive with waves stirred up from an armada of gators heading your way. The fleet would stop short of the shoreline and wait for someone to toss in something yummy to eat. Then, a wild feeding frenzy erupted before your eyes as tails splashed and rows of jagged teeth gnashed as they fought over the evening treats from the humans. I had nothing for them, so the lake remained calm.

The only gator I needed to watch out for was Old One Eye. Estimated to be a good fourteen feet long and weighed over a thousand pounds, no other gator messed with him. When he coasted in, it was like a battleship coming into Port. There was a parting of the reptilian fleet that would have made Moses jealous. He must have lost an eye in a fight with another gator years ago. Old One Eye hadn't lost that battle since there wasn't another gator close to his size in the lake.

With any luck, the massive reptile would be hanging around nearby. I could jump in and let him rip me apart. Being a local, I knew that wouldn't happen, but it distracted my state of mind.

As I stood there looking over Lake Alice, the parade slowly passed behind me. An hour passed by before I left. On my way off the peninsula, I spotted Old One Eye. Floating under the shade of a cypress tree a few feet from shore, he looked at me with his good eye. It was as if he was saying, "Be cool dude. Everything will work out. Oh, and bring me some chicken next time."

I must have been delusional as I was talking to an alligator!

# 41

## KRISTINA

The float passed by Lake Alice. Staring straight forward, Kristina tried to think of an excuse not to go to the game with Chip. He was a nice guy, but she wanted to go home. She felt heartache and sorrow for Helgi.

*Will I ever see Helgi again?*

Chip brushed against her, shifting attention back to him. "That was fun. Thanks for letting me ride along," Kristina politely said.

"I'm glad you came. Would you like something to eat?" Chip asked as they moved to the back of the float to get off.

"Well, maybe a bite. I need to get home." She wasn't hungry, but she had no reason to be rude to him.

# 42

# CHIP

Chip sensed something was wrong, but was glad Kristina agreed to spend more time with him. He wanted to get her back to his frat house.

"Cool. Let's go," he said.

He had a goal and worked his plan like an experienced predator. Chip had a bet to win. Getting her inside the frat house was step one.

Jumping off the float, Chip turned to help Kristina down. Reaching up with both arms he grabbed her by the waist and pulled her down against his body. For a few seconds they were face to face. When he leaned forward to kiss her, she twisted her head at the last second resulting in an awkward peck on the cheek.

*Playing coy are we. Ok, I'll play along.*

The Chipster was like a shark circling its prey. Tightening the circle with every pass. Getting closer and closer.

# 43

# KRISTINA

Frat Row bustled with homecoming festivities. Drinking continued with students gathered on balconies and front lawns. Respective floats sat in front of each frat house. Like a scene from *Animal House*, John Belushi would have fit right in. Nothing compared to this from her protected suburban life. Wide-eyed and overwhelmed, she was nervous, but intrigued. She felt way out of her league and sensed the wild, uncensored behavior of the frats.

"You seem to have a cheering squad," she said. "What are they egging you on for?" she asked.

She knew they were pushing the two of them together, but for some reason, she experienced a feeling of exhilaration by asking the obvious. Logic and caution gave way to flirting with Chip. Her uncharacteristic behavior muted her renewed feelings for Helgi.

Kristina glanced at Chip who grinned and acknowledged the shouts and whistles from his frat brothers. Several gave him a thumbs-up.

"Don't pay them any attention. They're just drunk," Chip deflected.

She flinched when Chip took her hand and squeezed, drawing her closer to his side. His relaxed smile sent a shiver through her body.

*He's nice. I think he likes me.*

## 44

## CHIP

Chip and Kristina walked past the huge, gaudy, lion statues that guarded the entrance to his frat house. Inside, were trays of sandwiches, bowls of chips and kegs of beer.

"Here, let's get you a plate," Chip said. *I have to at least pretend to be a gentleman.*

"Thanks," she replied, taking half a turkey sub and some chips.

"Beer?" he asked, hoping to ply her with some alcohol.

"No thanks. Do you have water?"

"What's that?" he said jokingly.

"Ha ha." Kristina gave him a weak laugh. "No, really I'm thirsty."

Chip stared at her a moment, assessing this girl he planned to seduce. "How about a soda? We have Coke or Sprite."

"Coke."

He pulled a can out of an ice-filled tub, popped the top and handed it to Kristina.

"Thanks. This is a nice place."

Chip nodded. "It's been here a long time. Has a great tradition. I'll show you around." He took her by the hand and gave her a tour starting in the large central living area, through the kitchen and then down a hall to a bedroom.

He stood at the door, pushing it open. "This is my room. Come on in," he said with the slyness of the Big Bad Wolf.

# 45

# KRISTINA

Kristina stopped in the doorway. She might have been naive, but that uneasy feeling she had about him before popped up again. She stood there, plate in one hand and the coke in the other. "Um, it looks nice," she said, biding her time.

"Come over here. The view from my window is great. You can see Lake Alice."

"I need to get going. Where can I toss my plate?" she said turning to look the way they'd come. She waited while he seemed to consider a reply.

"Oh, right this way. Here, I'll show you."

As Chip stepped into the hall, he slid his arm around her waist and walked her back to the living room. Kristina's emotions were in turmoil. Relieved that he didn't press her to come into his room, she also had a curious reaction to his arms around her. Her face flushed. Purely physical, her body's response to Chip's intimate embrace shocked Kristina. She felt betrayed by sensations that welled from deep inside and spread a familiar heat through her. *Should I be feeling this way?* He nudged her tighter and she grew warmer. *I can't control it!* When they reached the front door of the frat house, she turned to say goodbye. "Thanks for lunch and the ride on the float. I had a great time."

"I had fun too," he said. With his arm around her Chip leaned forward and gave her a friendly little kiss on the lips.

Surprised and still trying to sort out her feelings, she accepted it.

"See you in class?" he asked.

"Yeah, see you next week," she said and made her way down the sidewalk that would take her back to the commuter lot. Her head swam with thoughts of Chip, her reaction to his touch, his kiss, and her feelings toward Helgi.

# 46

# CHIP

Chip's mind was in full gear. *I'll need to be patient to reel in this one. If I push too hard, things might go badly.*

He didn't insist she stay but noticed her blush when he slipped his arm around her. Letting him kiss her sealed her fate. Chip watched Kristina walk away with a sense of accomplishment and a cocky smirk on his face.

*I'm going to win the bet.*

# 47

# KRISTINA

Kristina once again searched all over campus for Helgi. She'd spent extra time in the library on the weekends and between classes. Walked aimlessly between the business school and engineering. Parked on a bench near the bus stop at the GPA building, Kristina watched each student file off the commuter bus one by one. It caused her heartbreak every time it wasn't Helgi. She even had a mush lunch with the Krishna's on the plaza. All to no avail.

Pondering her dilemma while the Krishnas broke into a post mush chanting session, she noticed a phone booth next to the library.

*I could call the motel.*

She got up her nerve, found a dime in her purse and walked over to the booth. Picking up the heavy phone book attached to the booth by a wire cable, she opened up the yellow pages to motels. Finding the ad for the Florida Motel she dropped the dime in the slot and dialed the number.

The phone rang in her ear. No one picked up. The ringing continued. Kristina was about to hang up when there was a loud crackle and the ringing stopped. It sounded like someone put their hand over the receiver.

"I'll be with you in a minute sir. Helgi, number eight needs toiletries."

Kristina's heart jumped into her throat. He was there!

"Okay, I'll run it right over." She could hear in a muffled tone.

*Oh god, its Helgi.* She almost jumped in the phone booth.

"Florida Motel, can you hold please?" a lady asked.

"Ah…"

Before Kristina had a chance to respond the lady put her on hold. The phone went quiet, but for an occasional crackle that sounded like static electricity. Her heart pounded in her chest. Would he come to the phone, or would the lady say he wasn't there? Every negative thought ran through her mind. She wanted Helgi to answer but she was scared to death if he did.

Kristina tried waiting for someone to pick up, but the anxiety became too much for her. She lost her nerve and hung up.

She decided she had to talk to him in person. To see his face. No matter what words he spoke, she would know for certain how he felt about her by his expression…his eyes.

*I must find him. But how? The Halloween Ball! Maybe he'll be there.*

Normally, Kristina wouldn't be caught dead at the Ball. She knew of its reputation from high school friends who snuck into drink and party with the college students. It would be out of character for her to go, but she had no other choice except driving to the "wrong" side of town to the Florida Motel. She had never driven anywhere other than from home to campus and back.

But she wasn't in a normal state of mind. She thought about asking Chip to escort her to be safe.

Her usual clear-headed judgment was out of whack. Clouded by her desperation to find Helgi and her own insecurities…about who she was that kept them apart. Those same insecurities caused her to let her guard down and naively trust Chip. She never thought about how he would interpret her request. She wouldn't drive down to the motel, but somehow justified in her mind it was acceptable to go to the Halloween Ball with another guy, hoping to run into Helgi.

Love had scrambled her logical brain.

*I wonder if Chip would dress up as something nice with me.*

48

# HELGI

"Helgi, we were full last night and have a lot of checkouts this morning. Could you help Hester with the rooms?" Mom directed more than asked.

"Sure." I said in a monotone.

"What's the problem, Helgi? You seem down."

"Nothing, I responded while pushing open the office door. It seemed heavier than usual. But it wasn't the door. It was me. I was depressed and exhausted. The sight of Kristina with that frat boy on the float had taken everything out of me. I didn't give a shit about anything, not even going back to school for spring semester.

Gathering a pile of sheets from the laundry room, I plodded over to where Hester was working.

"Morn'n, baby."

"Hey," fell out of my mouth and onto the floor.

Hester saw the look on my face. She knew this was about Kristina. She'd been around this block too many times herself.

"What be happinen?" she asked, looking straight at

me while coming to a complete stop in the room. Hester never quit moving while cleaning. She would sing, impart worldly advice, take instructions from Mom and never stopped for a minute. But she sensed something was wrong and would not let me off until I came clean. She cared about me like a brother. At first, I tried to feign nonchalance.

"Nothing," I whimpered.

"Baby, don't be tryin' to fool ol Hester."

That's all it took for my emotional dam to burst. I told her everything as we went through the motions of cleaning rooms. She listened with a few "ahums" interjected here and there. Her deep empathetic sigh let me know she could hear the pain in my voice. I did my best to maintain composure and not cry. But the water in my eyes gave me away. When she turned aside, I wiped the tears on the sleeve of my shirt.

"Now lisin here. All you saw is what you saw. Don't be jumpin' to what you thinks you saw. Was she holdin' on to him or was he holdin' on to her?"

"Why, what difference does it make? They were together on the float, and he was touching her," I said, bringing my head up with a glimmer of hope.

"Makes a big difference, baby. Dudes like to show off. They wants to be the cock on the walk and tell the other brothers they gots the girl. It always be bout them. Like a lion stakin' claim over his pride."

"So, what's your point?" My posture straightened.

"Remember what I told you bout female dogs? How it be the bitches that choose their mate, not the studs?" Hester gave me a look as if to say this is important.

"Yes, I remember."

"You don't know if this girl, Ms. Kristina, done picked that other boy."

"Yes, but…"

"No buts, Helgi. You don't know what she be thinkin' or feelin'."

Wow, Hester never calls me by my real name. She must be serious.

"Only way to know for sure is to talk to her." Hester planted one hand on her hip and pointed a finger at me with the other. "So, you lisin to me. You go back up to campus, find Ms. Kristina and tells her how you feel."

"But what if she says she likes him and not me?"

"Well,"—Hester turned to strip the linens off another bed— "then you knows for sure. Won't make you feel any better, but you be feelin' bad anyway. Iffen she likes you more, then you be happy again. She be doing the pickin', not you, or that Frat boy. Iffen' you be the one to lettin' her choose, and he be the one tryin' to stake his claim over her, I promise you on my mammy's grave, Ms. Kristina be picking you." Hester stopped tugging at the sheets to look at me. "You understands, baby?"

"I think so, but I'm not sure I believe it," I said handing her some fresh towels.

Hester shot me a look that said, "Never question me about relationships!"

We continued cleaning the rooms while I pondered her words of wisdom. The thought of talking to Kristina about the parade, seeing her with that guy, and telling her that how I felt about her scared me to death. It would be easier to walk away. Forget it ever happened. Forget about Commuter Girl. But the pain of losing her, the raging fire in my blood at the thought of her and Frat boy together was unbearable. I couldn't live with either option. Maybe the motel was my destiny. Maybe I should embrace it and not fight it anymore. *Maybe* it wasn't such a bad life. Number Nine drove me crazy, but at least he didn't hurt me. Nor did screaming naked ladies, hookers, or cleaning the band's rooms filled with gross hidden surprises. I felt trapped by something I never expected; a girl was holding me captive, not the Florida Motel.

# 49

# HELGI

As Fall semester moved along, I kept myself busy helping at the motel. Dad was back on his feet and everything had returned to normal. Well, almost. We now locked the office door before sunset, not after. As darkness approached, the clunking noise of the oversized deadbolt landing in the metal doorframe reminded us of the robbery. Dad had installed a light in the corner where Shotgun Guy had hidden. With each passing night, the sound of the lock sliding into place was less noticeable. Eventually, it would dissolve into our routine.

I hadn't returned to campus in direct violation of Professor Hester's orders. Still, not a day passed without my thinking of Kristina.

"Helgi, isn't that big Halloween party coming up soon? You know, the one on campus?" Grandma asked, while doing the books.

"It's this weekend. Why?" I said, flipping one of the large switchboard jacks back and forth in my hand to pass the time. With nothing to study, desk duty became boring as hell. It was only moderately interesting when several customers drove up at the same time. Of course, that's when the switchboard, which had been silent all day, would light up. It's as if guests would watch the office from their rooms for cars to turn in and then call the front desk for some towels or an outside line to order a pizza. Still, being crazy busy was better than the hours of silence watching cars pass by on the road. I always wondered where everyone was going and why they were in such a hurry.

"Are you going this year?" Grandma asked.

"Hadn't thought about it."

"I think you should go. You need to get out of here and have some fun. 'All work and no play…'"

"I have no one to go with."

"Well, maybe you'll meet someone nice."

That's Grandma for you. The eternal optimist. But meeting *someone nice* at the Halloween Ball was like finding a virgin hooker at the motel. The event was an exercise in debauchery. Picture a huge bottle opener that popped the top off every inhibition of every student, all at the same time. The costumes ranged from sci-fi and horror to characters from the Wizard of Oz or Saturday Night Fever. A sexual theme ran through most of the creations. The Ball was always held on the Plaza of the Americas, and the student union usually booked a headline band for the event. Each year, the otherwise tranquil plaza would be transformed into one great big outdoor party. Booze flowed, joints burned and loud, I mean deafening, music from the band shook the stone walls of the old libraries right down to their foundations. Students did everything and everyone on the plaza during the Halloween Ball.

*Hmmm, it could be fun. Wouldn't know anyone. Could blow off a little steam. Maybe get shitfaced. Hell, I could get FUBAR!*

"I'll think about it," I said.

"Good. What will you go as?" She asked, head down, pencil in hand, eyes focused on the green debit and credit ledger sheet.

"I don't know; I'll come up with something."

My mind tossed around ideas. I wanted to blend in with the crowd.

*Condoms! That's it. I'll go as a giant box of condoms. Let's see, what kind? Trojans? Nah, they're like Chevys. Too common. Natural Lambs by FOUREX, that's the ticket. FOUREX says I've got style.* The most expensive rubbers available, Natural Lambs were like driving a Porsche—There was no substitute.

So, I had decided to go as a ginormous box of the best rubbers money could buy. Brilliant! Now all I needed to do was make the costume. FOUREX condoms came in a brown package with white lettering. We'd received an order of new pillows packed in large flat boxes. I'd thrown the boxes in the garbage. I rifled through the dumpster and found one still in good shape. Nothing gooey had spilled on it. I carried it over to the shed where we kept the riding mower and other maintenance stuff. Luckily, we had a gallon of brown, *interior latex* paint. The irony escaped me.

After cutting holes on each of the narrow sides for my arms and one in the center of the top for my head, I painted the entire box with the brown paint. While waiting for it to dry, I went to the laundry room to get a small plastic trash bag. They were clear, like a condom.

Rolling it up from the open end made it look like a giant, rolled-up rubber. All I needed was something to hold it on my head and to create…um…the reservoir.

*Let me see, what can I use? A bungee cord? No. Too big and heavy. Maybe some twine. Wait…one of Mom's headbands.* She used them to pull up her hair when she lathered cold cream all over her face before bed.

Trash bag in hand, I scurried through the kitchen into the bathroom and shut the door, so no one would see me trying on my condom cap. I placed the faux condom on my head, but it was too big. Figures! Yet another hit to my fragile ego.

I found a hairband in the bathroom cabinet drawer. Gathering up the excess bag, I tied it in place like a ponytail. Then, I pulled the top of the bag through Mom's headband and rolled it down near the top of my head. There looking back at me from the mirror was a new superhero: Condom Man. Protector from the dicks of the world!

In my haste to finish painting my box-o-rubbers, I forgot to remove the condom cap as I dashed through the kitchen. Grandma was taking a lunch break. Shocked by the sight of Condom Man, her dentures fell out of her gaping mouth and remained firmly sunk into her PB&J sandwich.

"Hey, Grandma. Thanks for reminding me about the Halloween Ball," I said, as I raced past her on my way out to the shed.

Bug-eyed, she sat there holding the denture-eating sandwich in front of her gapping toothless mouth.

Rummaging through the shed, I grabbed a can of white paint, a two-inch trim brush, and lettered the big brown box. Finished, I stepped back to admire my creation.

On the front it read: **FOUREX NATURAL LAMBS THE SUPER RUBBER!**

On the back: **SCREW YOUR NUTS OFF WITH FOUREX!**

Once the paint was dry, I shoved everything into the trunk of my car. I'm sure Grandma hadn't considered a giant box of condoms for my costume, but she managed to help me get my mind off Kristina and my head out of my ass.

"Thanks, Grandma. I'm going to the Halloween Ball," I said, entering the office for the afternoon shift with a spring in my step and smile on my face. I was pumped up and ready to party.

Grandma had collected herself, finished lunch and returned to working on the books at the front desk.

"You're welcome, Helgi," she said, adjusting her dentures with one hand while making entries with the other. She didn't comment on my condom cap. It was business as usual. That's what I loved about my little Finnish granny. She never judged anyone for anything.

Settling in for a quiet afternoon in the office with Grandma at my side and Hester cleaning rooms, I looked forward to a loud, raunchy, drink fest at the Ball.

# 50

# HELGI

It was already dark when I pulled into the commuter lot. A cold front had moved through, and the temperature had dropped into the low forties. Good thing, as my condom costume with rubber hat retained body heat. Any warmer, and I would have been a sweaty prophylactic mess. It was about eight thirty and the party was getting started. Shuffling my way up the hill, I cut through the Reitz Union and behind the journalism building. More and more costumed students funneled into the path leading to the plaza. Mummies, zombies, aliens, Beetle Juice, Luke Skywalkers, Princess Leas, Yodas and several Ferris Buellers, all marched side by side.

*Oh look, coeds dressed as hookers. Seems redundant.*

As the caravan of creatures and characters approached the Ball, the volume of the band increased exponentially with each step. Commander Cody and His Lost Planet Airmen were belting out some classic rock. The lyrics were as raunchy as the students' costumes and emboldened them to act out their Halloween personas. There was a couple clothed as a giant penis and vagina gyrating in and out of each other to the beat of the music. But that paled compared to the parade-float-sized erection making its way through the crowd. Handled by multiple dorm rats, they had ingeniously rigged a contraption to shoot milk out the end, drenching anyone caught in the line of fire. The hooker coeds got right in front and intentionally took it in the face.

*How original!*

I was getting a good buzz on from a bottle of Jack being passed around when I looked up and saw a couple dressed as Raggedy Ann and Andy. There was something familiar about Raggedy Ann. I moved in closer. Andy was holding a beer and talking to Darth Vader when Ann turned in my direction. It was Kristina. With the reservoir tip of my condom cap flopped to one side, we stood facing each other. A giant box of FOUREX rubbers with a forlorn face looking into Raggedy Ann's eyes. We said nothing. Music blared over us and time seemed to stop with everyone around us in suspended animation—the band muted to a muffled noise in the background.

Then, Andy put his arm around her and pulled her away. Motionless in my big brown box, hands at my side, limp tip on my head, I watched them fold into the drunken swarm. Commander Cody jolted me back to reality like audible smelling salts. I turned away and started walking back to the commuter lot. It was the homecoming parade all over again.

Zombielike, I missed the turn at North South Drive. Before I knew it, I was out on the peninsula in Lake Alice. If not for the reflection of the moon off the water's surface, I would have fallen in. Not a good thing, since alligators feed at night. Even standing on the shore was dangerous. Alligators can leap out of the water with a single thrust of their powerful tails to capture unsuspecting prey too close to the shoreline. My eyes, burning from all the pot smoke at the Ball, scanned the lake. Finding Old One Eye was all that mattered. He was the only gator big enough to grab me, condom box and all, and drag me under.

My mind was reeling. Jerk didn't know I had opened the door for him. That it was me who had shown her there was more to life than work and school. "You're welcome you frat fuck," I said angrily over the lake.

*Hurt her, and I will kick your pasty east coast ass back to Nantucket. Better yet, I'll introduce you to this guy I know from the hood. He only has half an ass, but he can still twist you into a human pretzel and have you running back home to your mommy, crapping in your khaki's the entire way.*

## 51

## CHIP

Chip had been only too happy to oblige Kristina's request to take her to the Halloween Ball. Ecstatic and emboldened when she asked, it was the perfect setting to get her in the right mindset and close the deal. What better place than a raunchy party with the primary theme of open and free sex? *She wants to be with me. She wants to hook up.* Kristina was easy prey. What girl in her right mind *wouldn't* want to be with him, especially some local chick?

He kept reeling her in by agreeing to dress up as Raggedy Andy. The ribbing he took from his frat brothers was worth getting her into bed and winning the bet.

"I'd like to go now," Kristina said as Chip guided her through the crowd.

"You say something, sweetie?" he asked cupping a hand around his ear.

"I want to go home," she shouted over the deafening music.

"But we just got here," Chip whined.

"I know. I'm sorry."

"Let's stay for one more song by the Commander."

"You can stay, but I'm going now."

Chip thought about his goal and the bet. Having gained her trust, he wasn't about to blow it now.

"Okay, okay. I'll walk you back to the fraternity and give you a ride to your car. It's a little crazy out here. You don't want to be walking alone on campus tonight," he said.

Taking her by the hand, he led her through the crowd of revelers, off the plaza and headed down Stadium Road to Frat Row.

# 52

## KRISTINA

The cold night air was moist and heavy. Kristina could see her breath as she exhaled. The only reason she agreed to let Chip escort her to the Ball was the hope she would run into Helgi. Unfortunately, she did. The look on Helgi's face showed how much she'd hurt him. It wasn't what she planned and felt terrible.

Kristina let Chip hold her hand as they walked through campus to his frat house. She felt nothing romantic for him. But he'd been a gentleman, and she didn't want to hurt his feelings too.

"We're back. Come in and get out of the cold while I get my keys," he said, leading her into the frat house and down the hall to his room. He opened the door and ushered her in.

Kristina's mind was on Helgi, seeing him, the look on his face. She had let her guard down.

Uneasy about being in his bedroom with all his frat brothers still at the Ball, Kristina turned to wait in the hall. Before she could leave, Chip grasped her wrist and yanked her back. Wrapping his arms around her waist, he kissed her hard, pressing his tongue between her pursed lips and deep into her mouth. Kristina turned away breaking the kiss, but her head landed on his shoulder as he forcefully pulled her closer. Her hands got trapped between their bodies.

"Please stop, Chip."

Continuing to grope and fondle her, he brushed her hair aside and began licking and sucking her neck while grinding his pelvis into hers. Then he slid his hands under her costume and down her backside. Groping her behind over her panties Kristina pushed him off with all her strength.

"Chip, no, stop it!"

"Were alone, no one's going to catch us," he stated with arrogance while wrapping his arms around her again. "You know you want it."

"No, Chip. I don't want to do this." She kneed him hard in the groin, ran out of his room and down the hall.

Glancing back, she saw an enraged Raggedy Andy bounding after her, thick red yarn wig flopping from side to side. Baggy blue overalls chafing between his legs, he looked like a mad clown from a horror movie chasing down his prey while grasping his nuts with both hands.

Kristina stumbled out the front of the frat house. She didn't know where to go, but knew she had to get away. Terrified, she ran down the hill straight to Lake Alice.

"Kristina, stop!" Chip commanded in pursuit.

"Help!" she cried out, hoping someone…anyone would be close by. "Help me!"

# 53

## HELGI

"Help me!" Someone screamed from Frat Row. When I turned to see what all the commotion was about, I saw Raggedy Ann running straight toward me with Andy in hot pursuit. He was closing the gap between them fast. Kristina ran past me gasping for breath and crying hysterically. The fear in her voice seared my senses like a red-hot branding iron on bare flesh. My blood boiled as I came up from the water's edge to the path around the lake. The cardboard box of my costume restricted my legs to an awkward running shuffle.

"Come back here, you teasing little bitch!" Raggedy Andy shouted as he approached my position.

That's all I needed to hear. Adrenaline surged through my body. Stepping into the path between the running Raggedies, Arms protruding from the sides of the condom box, I clenched my fists, swung hard with a left, and punched the jerk in the face. He went down hard, landing flat on his back with a loud, painful grunt.

"OW! Shit! What the hell?" Appearing stunned at the sight of a giant box of condoms standing over him, Raggedy Andy gained his senses, scrambled backward and got to his feet.

"You little fucker. Who do you think you are? Get the hell out of my way," the Andy barked.

"What's it look like, asswipe? I'm her *protection*. Leave her alone, you raggedy little prick." Enraged by both Kristina's rebuke and getting decked out of nowhere, he ran straight at me. Raggedy Andy took a flying leap right into the FOUREX box. The force pushed us both back to the edge of the lake. I landed on my back with Raggedy Andy on top of me. He walloped away with everything he had. It was hard to hit me through the big brown box, so he went for my face.

Kristina had stopped running. "Helgi!"

I craned my neck to get away from Punching Andy. Looking upside down over the lake, I saw multiple pairs of eyes poking out of the water glowing iridescent red from the moonlight. Gators. Lots of them. Slithered through the water toward the commotion on the shore.

I was about to maneuver to one side to gain some leverage when I heard Kristina yell, "Get off him, Chip Leave him alone!" at the same time she jumped on his back and started scratching at his eyes. Now I had both Raggedies piled on top of me. It took everything I had to breathe under the crushing weight. My condom box crumpled like an accordion. All the while, a flotilla of red eyes moved closer and closer to the fight. Finally, with one big heave, I pushed off from the high side of the bank. With Kristina pulling Chip from behind the pile became top heavy. I gained the upper hand and pushed them off. Both Raggedy Ann and

Andy toppled over, rolled through the dirt and down the bank. I grabbed Kristina before she hit the water.

Chip rolled straight into the murky, cold water of Lake Alice.

"Get behind me," I yelled to Kristina, flailing my arms backward from the sides of the condom box.

Moving down to where Chip floundered in the muck, I spotted a chicken leg in the moonlight. Covered in dirt. It must have been dropped by someone feeding the gators. The dirt prevented the them from smelling the chicken and coming out to eat it. I picked it up, put my foot on Andy's chest to hold him down and stuffed the chicken leg down his overalls. Just then he grabbed my ankle and pulled me into the lake, clawing and smashing at me. The FOUREX box took the brunt of his attack but started tearing apart and turning to mush from the water. Ironically, my condom box was now protecting me.

I knew all the commotion would attract the gators. We sounded like a wounded animal thrashing in the water. I was more worried about getting chomped by a gator than the limp flailing's I was taking from this wimp ass frat boy. An actual Raggedy Andy could have put up a better fight. With an angry push of my leg, I shoved Chip further offshore. His feet sunk into the slippery muck holding him hostage in the lake.

"Look around, asshole. There are gators everywhere and you smell like chicken. Bet you'll taste like it when they chomp your raggedy ass!"

I had the high ground and could easily have kicked him back in if he tried to escape. The alligators were almost on him when they all abruptly stopped, did an immediate about face and swam off to the center of the lake. Just then I saw a great big glowing eye, rushing full steam ahead like a battleship straight toward Chip. The gator was hungry and wanted chicken and Chips for dinner.

"Oh, shit."

"*What?*" Chip said his voice shaky with terror.

"It's Old One Eye, and he's coming for you," I said with mixed emotions. He deserved to have the shit scared out of him. But this was a huge bull gator, and he could have easily ripped him in half with his powerful jaws and rows of prehistoric teeth. Then he'd drag him under and keep Chip's remains there for late night snacks. This was now a very serious and dangerous situation…at least for the Chipster.

"Oh, God, please help me!" Chip begged.

"What was that? I didn't hear what you said," I asked snidely, knowing I had a few more seconds to mess with him.

"Please! I'll do anything. Don't let him eat me!"

"Give me your hand," I said giving in to common sense. Besides, I'd lose a tug o' war with this monster at one end of Chip and me on the other.

I pulled him out of the water and stood him upright in front of me. Holding him with both hands by the front of his mud-covered Andy overalls, I leaned the Chipster backward over the water. The huge gator lurked a few feet offshore.

"You leave her alone or I'll toss your ass back in. Understand you little prick?"

Chip nodded a meek "yes" of defeat as his dripping wet Andy wig bled all over his costume.

I swung him around and tossed him up the bank. The Chipster stumbled along the ground before catching his balance and running back to his frat house.

Kristina jumped up and threw her arms around my neck.

"Helgi, I was so scared." Her body shook as she sobbed into my condom cap.

The anger and adrenaline in me instantly evaporated. In its place welled up joy, happiness and relief. Her embrace ignited the most powerful feeling I'd ever experienced. A feeling I had never felt for girl in my life. I was in love with Kristina.

# 54

# HELGI

So, there we stood, Raggedy Ann covered in dirt and a mushy wet box of rubbers topped with a limp condom cap leaning to one side. Only the remaining letters of my costume were REX on the front and SCREW on the back.

"He won't bother you anymore," I said. "Can I walk you to your car?"

"Sure," she said, slipping down the crushed condom box back to the ground.

As we turned to walk away from Lake Alice, I spotted Old One Eye. I could've sworn he winked at me. This time, as if to say, "Not bad for a local boy. If that creep bothers her again, toss 'im back in the lake. I'd love some chicken-fried frat for dinner."

Dirty Ann and SCREWREX began walking side by side down Museum Road back to the commuter lot.

"What happened, Helgi? Why did you disappear?" Kristina asked.

"It's a long story," I said.

"It's a long walk to the cars." Kristina tilted her head toward me and smiled.

On the way, I told her about the robbery, Dad getting hurt, and my dropping classes to help run the motel.

"That's terrible, Helgi. I'm so sorry about your dad."

"It's okay. He's better now."

"Helgi, about Chip…"

"You don't have to explain. It's none of my business. I'm happy I ran into you tonight."

"I thank God you were here," she said with relief and joy in her voice.

Turning down North South Drive we could hear the thumping of Commander Cody in the distance. The rumble of the Halloween Ball rolled through campus and spilled out over the commuter lot.

"Where's your car?" I asked.

"It's over there next to that blue Road Runner," Kristina pointed to my car.

"The burgundy Mustang?" My heart skipped.

"Yes, why?"

"I've seen it before. That blue Road Runner is mine."

"Cool car," we said simultaneously, looking into each other's eyes.

Then a wall of awkwardness suddenly rose between us. The sight of her and Chip on the float still stung. I couldn't deny my feelings for her, but I couldn't bring myself to tell her. I said nothing.

"Well…see you around campus sometime?" she asked, breaking the silence.

"Sure, I should be back next semester," I said.

"Okay, well…thanks again for coming to my rescue." Then she reached up over my drenched costume and kissed me. Confused, jealous and hurt, my mind reeled. But her kiss stirred the fire and passion I still felt for her. With a somber look, Kristina reluctantly turned and got in her car.

I didn't care if it wasn't the right time. I had to tell her how I felt. Besides, if I didn't say anything, Hester would kill me. But it was too late. Kristina had already backed out of her parking space and was slowly heading toward the entrance. The pit of my stomach ached as the Mustang pulled out of the Commuter Lot.

*What the hell is wrong with you, man? You friggin' idiot! Crap, Hester's will kill me if she finds out.*

In the distance the married housing bus passed by on its last run for the night.

# 55

## KRISTINA

Kristina's eyes welled up as she pulled away. She didn't want it to end this way. Something deep in her heart told her Helgi was her soul mate.

Shifting into drive, she let the Stang move away at idle speed. She could barely see him in the rearview mirror through the blur of tears filling her eyes.

*Should I stop and tell him how I feel?* "Please, Helgi, wave at me, yell, run, jump, do anything to stop me. I love…" she pleaded out loud. Sorrow invaded her heart. Gripping the steering wheel, she wanted to turn around, but the fear that he didn't want to see her anymore stopped her. Her chest tightened at the sight of him standing by his car watching her drive away. Kristina turned out of the commuter lot, then stopped at the intersection of Museum Road and North South Drive to pull herself together. A couple dressed as Mark Anthony and Cleopatra stepped off the married housing bus and joined hands for the walk up the hill. She burst into tears and sobbed all the way home.

## 56

## KRISTINA

Sitting at her desk, Kristina blankly starred out her bedroom window. Unable to concentrate on her assignments since Chip's attack and the big fight at Lake Alice. She felt ashamed, embarrassed and lost. Her world had been turned upside down. Her dad walked by her bedroom on his way out to the garage. He always spent Saturday mornings piddling out in the garage. It was his way of decompressing from work. Kristina loved hanging out with him and especially working on her Mustang. In a way, she way her father's son.

Poking his head in the door, "Want to help me change the oil in the '67?" he asked.

"No thanks,"

"What's up?"

"Nothing. I just need to catch up on my homework," she fibbed.

She never had to catch up with homework, so he knew something was wrong. "I could really use an extra set of hands," he persisted.

"Well, okay. It is past 5000 miles since the last change."

"That's my girl."

She closed her books and followed him out to the garage.

"Back your car out while I get the ramps." Her dad treated her like an adult and trusted her with practically anything he could do. She never felt like he treated her different because she was a girl. When he had the ramps aligned in front of the wheels, he used hand gestures to guide her forward. He had taught her how to slowly approach the ramps, feel the contact by the tires, then use just enough gas to drive the car up and on top, but not too much so she could stop before running off the ends. Kristina loved spending time with her dad. The rest of the world and all its stresses didn't exist when they were working together on some project in the garage. It was his happy place and she was happy he shared it with her.

Kristina opened and assembled the oil cans on the workbench while her dad slid on a car creeper under the engine to drain the old oil. While lying under the car, he dug a little deeper.

"What's the scoop, baby girl?" he asked.

"Baby girl" was all it took. It was like kryptonite to Kristina. Tears welled up in her eyes and began dropping past the engine, splattering on the concrete driveway next to his head. He had hit a nerve.

"Oh, Daddy," she said through sobs.

"Ah hum." He listened but said nothing.

"I made a mistake. I was with that frat boy on the float in the parade."

"The one you told me invited you to work on their float?"

"Yes, Chip Cantwell. He's in my engineering classes."

"Now I remember. He sounds like a nice guy."

"Yeah, well…"

"Well what?"

"I saw Helgi saw at the… parade with Chip." Kristina caught herself. She couldn't bare telling her dad about the Halloween Ball, the attack by Chip and the fight with Helgi. Embarrassed and ashamed, this was the first time in her life she didn't tell her dad everything. She also feared he would go Frat Row and beat the crap out of Chip.

"I could see the hurt on his face."

"I thought Helgi was gone? You told me he up and disappeared."

"I know, but I can't get him off my mind. There's something special about him. I really like him Dad, I need to make it right."

"What about Chip?"

"Chips a pig."

"Okay..."

"Drain plug is back in. You can start pouring the new oil," he said. Kristina's dad had a way of letting her talk. He seemed to know when to push, when to back off and when she needed a distraction. It's one of the reasons she loved spending time with him in the garage. She wiped the tears on her sleeves and started pouring fresh oil through a funnel in the valve cover of the engine. Dad slid out from under the Mustang. Lying on the creeper he looked at his daughter.

"Baby girl, did you know Grandma didn't think I was good enough for your mother?"

"Really? No, I didn't know that."

"Yes, she'd give me a little smack on the back of my head every time I came over to visit."

"Grandma hit you?"

"Yeah, it didn't hurt, but I knew it wasn't a love tap. She even tried to fix your mom up with other boys she thought were better than me," he confessed.

"What did you do?" How did you win her over?" Kristina asked.

"I didn't. I assumed it was all over for us."

"So, what happened? How did you and Mom get together?" Kristina alternated her focus between her dad below and the empty oil cans as she replaced them with full ones and filled the crankcase.

"I'll let you in on a little secret, but you can't tell your mom I told you, okay?"

Kristina's eyes opened wide. Distracted by what her dad was saying, she spilled oil in the engine, and it dripped down to the driveway.

"Hey kiddo, you're spilling the oil."

"Oops, sorry," she said, redirecting the can over the funnel. "So, tell me the secret."

"Your mom came after me. She showed up on my porch one day and asked me out. This was a big deal back in those days. A girl asking out a boy, let alone one her mother didn't approve of."

"You're kidding! Mom asked you out?"

"Yup. I figured if I was good enough for your mom, I was good enough for Grandma. Didn't give a hoot what the old bat thought of me at that moment. I knew I loved your mom, and that's all that mattered," he said.

"But you and mom weren't strangers, how does that help me?" Kristina asked."

"Listen to me Kristina. If you really like this boy. If your heart is set on him, you need to do something about it. Tell him how you feel."

"What about all that stuff the nuns taught us about 'proper dating' and that 'good girls don't chase boys'?"

"Look, when it comes to teaching kids about dating, it's the parents that matter, not the Church and especially not the nuns!" he said emphatically.

Kristina was taken aback by his response.

*That was interesting. Sounds like Dad isn't a hundred percent on board with this Catholic guilt stuff.*

I'm scared Dad, "What if he won't talk to me? What if he's too hurt from seeing me with Chip at the ba… rade?" Kristina stumbled. *Whew, almost blew it again.*

"Trust me. If you show up at his front door, he'll melt for you like butter at a summer picnic. And if he doesn't, I'll give him a granny smack."

"Thanks, Daddy. I love you," she said, putting the cap on the valve cover and wiping off the spilled oil with an old rag.

"Love you too, baby girl."

The next morning Kristina awoke with a new resolve. She would fight for Helgi. If he wouldn't come after her, she would go after him. Nuns be damned.

# 57

# HELGI

I'd done nothing about seeing Kristina since the Halloween Ball. Still torn up about her and the Frat ass, I couldn't think straight. Also, fearing the wrath of Hester, I had avoided her all week. But that wouldn't last. She was way too smart not to know something was up with me. Thankfully I had made it to Saturday. I was safe for the weekend.

It was unseasonably warm, so I wore only a pair of shorts and tennis shoes for maid work. No shirt as, I never liked the feel of a sweaty t-shirt clinging to my skin. Cars came and went from the motel parking lot with their usual randomness. Nothing out of the ordinary had caught my attention when the phone rang in the room I was cleaning. It wasn't hard to figure out which one I was in, as the door was propped open by the USS Battlecart.

"Hi, Mom. What's up?

"You have a visitor here to see you. Says you invited her to use the pool sometime?"

I glanced outside and saw a burgundy Mustang parked by the office. My heart jumped.

"She says her name is Kristina Schmitt."

"Oh, my g…uh…yeah, I know her. She's in my English class," I said trying to be cool.

"Helgi, you didn't tell me about a girl. She's cute."

"Mom!

"Okay, I'll send her right over."

I hung up the phone and went to the door of room eight. There before my eyes, was Kristina. Her face beamed as she walked toward me. She wore a sheer cover-up, her slender, bikini-clad body coyly disguised underneath.

"Kristina," I said with over jubilance.

"Hi there. That invitation to hang out at your pool still stand?" she asked with a heartwarming smile.

"Absolutely. Make yourself at home. I've got a couple more rooms to clean and then I'll join you." It didn't dawn on me that the maid cat was out of the bag. She didn't seem to notice or care. "How'd you find me…I mean the motel?"

"Um, big blue sign that looks like Florida."

On the pretense of looking where she indicated with a thumb over her shoulder, I stepped outside.

I wanted to hug her. Kiss her. Hell, I wanted to take her into number eight and make love right on the spot.

"Cool, I'll be sunbathing by the pool," she said.

With Kristina waiting for me…in a bikini, my cleaning efficiency instantly doubled. Hester couldn't have done those rooms any faster. I sprayed the last one with air freshener, locked the door and energetically rolled the cart back to the laundry room. Dropping the keys on the front desk, I headed over to the pool before the Finnish CIA could interrogate me.

Approaching the pool my eyes were laser focused on Kristina lying stretched out on a chaise lounge. Her sheer cover-up, draped over the back of the chair, lightly fluttered in the afternoon breeze. Looking down at her, I admired every shapely rise and fall of her body. The tiny bikini top revealed the curve of her supple breasts, while the skintight bottoms held like a glove around her firm little rear and then fell gloriously down between her thighs.

*What a body!*

I kneeled beside her to remove my shoes.

"Ready for a swim?" I asked.

"Yeah, I'm hot. Let's get in," she said rising from the lounge.

She *was* hot. Oh man she was hot!

"Let's go." I said practically leaping from her side right into the pool. I hit the water with a splash, went down to the bottom and then broke the surface near the shallow end. Kristina jumped off the diving board. Breaking the surface, she swam across the pool and stood up in front of me.

"Whew, that feels good," she said, gathering up her long, flowing hair, now slickened over her head, and letting it fall to the small of her back. With both hands raised, her breasts stood straight out in my face.

"Yeah, I jump in several times a day. Everything we do around here seems to be done in the extreme heat of the day. Sorry I was sweating so much when you got here." I said while my eyes drank in the sight of her.

"I don't mind. You look good all shinny in those

shorts," Kristina said, moving closer. We drifted together, and I wrapped my arms around her. Half underwater and half above, our bodies pressed together. Kristina pulled my face to hers for a long, wet, passionate kiss. Not a little peck on the lips, yet not a gross tongue lashing to see if we still had tonsils. It was a kiss that said, "I love you." Under the surface my *passion* for her grew to the point there was no hiding it. Kristina kept kissing me. I pulled her closer. She started to slowly thrust her pelvis into mine. Our breathing became shallow and abrupt. Exhaling more than inhaling, I almost lost control when…

# 58

# HELGI

"Helgi!" Leena yelled across the parking lot. "Did you put da towels in da vashing machine?"

She couldn't see what was going on below the surface, but she wasn't stupid. The Finnish CIA had us under surveillance and knew all too well how fast her not-so-little boy could get into trouble. Kristina came across as a nice girl, but she did show up unannounced, wearing a bikini and asking for her boy. Mom might have thought she was some gold digger wanting to get her hands-on Sven and Leena's vast wealth of the Florida Motel. Ha,"vast wealth" and "the Florida Motel," now there's a stretch!"

Turning my head away from Kristina while she kept teasing me with her hips, I groaned back with irritation. "Yes, I put them in the washer."

"Okay, I'll go svitch dem," she said, walking over to the laundry room.

"Thanks," I squeaked. Kristina smirked at me and giggled.

"Well, that didn't spoil the mood now did it?" I said exasperated. My passion abated. Mom had metaphorically tossed cold water on us—and in a swimming pool no less.

"You want to try out the slide?" I said sheepishly.

"Sounds like fun," She replied and swam over to the stairs.

"Here, let me turn this hose on. It makes it slippery and cools it down."

"Spoken like a true pool boy," she said with a smirk.

Kristina climbed the steep ladder first, with me right behind in hot pursuit. Enjoying the view as we made our way up, I felt tightness in my shorts. Everything was back at full attention down there. *Oh boy, I hope Mom's still in the laundry room.*

We went down the slide a few times and then settled into some PG-rated, Mom-approved frolicking. Eventually, we hung on the side of the pool, heads perched on folded arms. We were talking when I noticed two familiar cars parked outside number fifteen. It was Casey Lockwood and Office-Hours Coed.

*Hmmm, what is he doing here on a Saturday? Guess a professor's got to do what a professor's got to do.*

"Hey, not to change the subject, but how's comp class going?" I asked her.

"Not too good. I lost my tutor, remember?" she said.

"Don't remind me. You going to pass?" I whispered, staring at the door to room fifteen.

"I'll probably get a C. It bugs me that English comp is going to hurt my GPA. How is it supposed to make me a better engineer?"

I could hear frustration in her voice. An evil plot

began developing in my brain. "I can help you get a better grade,"

"How?" she asked, cocking her head in my direction.

"You see that yellow MG Midget over there?"

Kristina pulled her head up and looked over the parking lot. Dr. Lockwood's room was about thirty feet away. "Yeah, looks like a 65' or 66.' Why?"

*I'm in love! She's gorgeous, smart and knows about cars. What more could a guy ask for?*

"Well, if my timing is right, the door to that room will open in a few minutes and someone we know will come out."

"Who?" Her interest piqued; Kristina looked like a meerkat staring from the side of the pool.

I didn't need help getting through Casey's class and wanted to do something nice for Kristina.

"Dr. Lockwood is in there right now with that coed who always sits in the front row.

"Dr. Lockwood from English comp?" she asked incredulously.

"Yup."

"How do you know?"

"He's one of our regulars. Comes here every Tuesday. Says he needs a quiet place to write, but recently he's been holding office hours with that coed."

"You're kidding me!"

"Nope."

"Does he know you live here? That your family owns the motel?"

"He knows but hasn't connected me to his class."

"What are you going to do?"

"We're about to get you an A in English comp," I said, the devil in my voice.

"But Helgi, that's not fair. I didn't earn it."

"Is it fair that coed is getting an A?"

"What? That's impossible!"

"Oh, it's possible alright. I sat close enough to her in class to see her grades on every paper. He gave her all A's!"

Kristina's brow furrowed and her faced squinched with anger. "That's wrong! What's your plan?" The tone of her voice instantly changed from innocent schoolgirl to Ninja warrior.

"Follow my lead," I said.

A few minutes later the door to number fifteen opened and out popped Casey and the coed.

"Right on cue," I mumbled.

Kristina's eyes bulged, watching as they stood next to the MG and the professor planted one last kiss on his student.

"Never seen him do that before."

"Do what?" Kristina whispered.

"Come out of the room together and make out in public. He's usually more discreet. Man, she's really got him wrapped around her little finger. Okay, you ready for operation GPA?"

"Yeah, let's do this," Kristina said rubbing her hands together.

I shouted across the parking lot from the pool, "Hey, Dr. Lockwood?"

The professor shoved Office Hours Coed ass backward into the little MG in a move to hide her behind his back. Shock and horror scorched his face red as he looked over to the pool.

Unabashed, I announced across the parking lot. “We’re in your English comp class.”

“Hi, Dr. Lockwood,” Kristina said as she tipped her head and waved at him.

“Nice touch with the wave,” I complimented, while maintaining eye contact with the professor.

The dumb blond waved back. “Hey, I know you,” she said, her gaze on me. “You sit behind me in class.”

Kristina rolled her eyes. “Really?” She might have been a tad jealous. I couldn’t have planned it any better.

“Now, make sure he knows your name,” I instructed. “Blondie said she knew me, but not you. He needs to put a name with a face.” With Office Hours Coed happily confirming our existence as students in his class, Casey was dead meat.

“Kristina Schmitt. I’m in your class too. Nice seeing you, Dr. Lockwood.”

“Wow, you’re good at this” I said with pride.

The professor gave us a cowering nod, said something to Blondie and hurried back to his room. Office Hours Coed hopped into the MG and waved at us as she pulled out.

“Now what?” Kristina asked.

“Simple, ask him for some help after class.”

“Should I flirt with him?” she asked tilting her head and batting her eyes at me.

“No! And DON’T agree to meet him at some damn motel for office hours!” I said with a stern look.

“What, are you jealous?” she asked while running her hand down my leg.

"No, he's no better than that frat boy. Worse, he has power."

"What makes you think he will do anything about my grade?"

"Trust me; there's only one thing more important to him."

"What's that?" she asked.

"Tenure. And believe me, rumors about meeting coeds in motel rooms will not go over well with the University. He wants to keep this under the covers…so to speak."

"Once again, you are my hero. Whatever can I do to thank you, Mr. Pool boy?" she said with a saucy southern accent. She blushed as if embarrassed by what she had said, but I wasn't going to let the opportunity go…not anymore. I owed that to myself…and Hester.

"Oh, I can think of several things you can do to… err…for me." Slipped out with a little too much ease. We had taken our banter to the next level.

"We need a place my mother can't spy on us," I said, turning toward her and running my hand down her back and gently cupping her rear. "Do you like canoeing?"

# 59

# KRISTINA

The closest Kristina had come to a canoe was visiting some family friends at their cabin on Orange Lake. They had one pulled up on the shore. While the adults talked around the grill and the other kids and ran around screaming for no particular reason, Kristina decided to go sit in the canoe and read a book. That was the extent of her nautical experience.

"What time is it?" she asked.

Helgi looked over to the office. There was a large clock on the wall behind the desk. From the pool, he could just make out the time.

"About 4 o'clock," he replied.

"It's 4 already? I need to get going. My folks will be worried if I'm late for dinner."

They got out of the pool, toweled off and Kristina put on her coverup.

"I'm really glad you came to see me," he said.

"Thanks for inviting me. I had fun."

"It was nice to see you, Kristina."

"Nice to see you too, Helgi."

He walked her to her car and opened the door like a gentleman. They paused and then kissed.

"See you soon?"

"I hope so." She said.

Pulling out of the motel she could see Helgi in the rearview mirror. Unlike the last time after the Halloween Ball, she felt warmth and joy. Her dad was right.

*Canoeing? And where did that southern accent come from? Stop. Don't care. I've got him back.*

# 60

# HELGI

"Mom, it looks like Dad is on the mend. You think I could go back to UF next semester?" I asked while organizing the room keys.

"Ya, your dad and I dink it's time. Ve can handle da motel now," she said.

*That's weird. If she's okay with me going back to UF, why is she speaking with her stress voice?*

Looking her straight in the eyes I asked, "Mom. Are you sure? Is everything all right?" I could see her eyes tearing up.

"Ya, Helgi, I'm yust going to miss you. It's been so nice having you around. Sven doesn't talk much, ya know. If it's not about business, he's more interested in vatching the boob tube," she acknowledged.

I heard what she wasn't saying. Mom was lonely. "You still have Grandma." I said.

"Grandma is nice, but she only vants to talk about da old country."

"Well, it's not like I'm moving out. I'll still be here to

help…and chat." I wanted to make her feel better. I had no idea she would miss me.

"You going to see dat girl again? Da vone dat came here to swim in da pool?" she asked.

"Kristina? I hope so. I like her, Mom…a lot." I blurted.

"She seems like a nice girl, but you be careful, Helgi. Don't knock her up."

"Mom!"

"I'm yust saying Helgi. I know how girls trap boys."

"She's not going to trap me. Besides, Kristina is special. I enjoy talking with her and hanging out." I said. I had shared my feelings with my mother like I did with Hester. "I'll treat her with respect and be kind to her like you taught me…and yes, I'll be careful."

"I know you vill," she said. But the tone in her voice had not changed.

"Okay, I'll head up to campus this afternoon to register for spring semester."

Mom was on my mind on the way up to the Bursar's office. I knew something was bothering her, and it wasn't being worried I'd knock up Kristina. It didn't sound like motherly protection. Then it hit me like a ton of bricks. Kristina threatened our relationship. For eighteen years, Mom had me all to herself. She was the only girl in my life, and now another was moving in on her turf. Kristina would take me away from my mother. Our time together. Our conversations. My heart sank as I turned into the parking lot. I had hurt Mom's feelings, because I had feelings for Kristina.

*Nice move Einstein! This girl stuff is complicated.*

The class enrollment line wrapped up and down

Anderson Hall. Forms filled out; the waiting game began. News of classes filling up flashed through the line like a wildfire pushed by winds up a mountainside. Some students even had backup classes ready on new forms ready to go to avoid starting all over at the back of the line. Overconfident or just lazy, I didn't bother with backup forms.

It was akin to standing in line at Disney—slowly moving back and forth, seeing the same people repeatedly, until you finally reach the last turn before getting on the ride.

"Econ 201 just closed," echoed through the crowd of anxious students. Groans of "crap, shit, damn it" poured forth every time a class closed. Not that there was only one of each class. Rather, it was the preferred time and day that would fill first. Who the hell wants to take chemistry or calculus on Fridays at 3 p.m.? And if a core requisite filled up, you either had to take a heavy load the next semester to catch up or, worse, delay graduation.

Looking over the horde, I spotted Kristina about a dozen students ahead of me. As the line turned, we made eye contact.

"Hey, fancy meeting you here," I said grinning like kid in a toy store.

*"Fancy meeting you here," what is this? The fifties?*

"Helgi, you're coming back to school?" Kristina shouted over the hundreds of students around us. Some took an interest in our conversation, but most continued their nervous fidgeting.

"Yeah, the folks said it's ok for me to start classes again. Dad's feeling much better now."

"That's great news. I'm so happy to see you."

Passing close enough to hug, our eyes locked together. As the line kept moving, now separating us, we continued talking—twisting our heads and then walking backward to maintain eye contact. I wasn't about to waste any more time, not one second. Making the turn at the far end I leaned out over the line, trying not to run into the people coming from the opposite direction.

"Hey, you are doing anything this Saturday?" I asked, lightly brushing her arm as we passed. The touch sent waves of heat through my skin.

"Nothing special," she replied. "What do you have in mind?"

"A picnic"

"At the motel?"

"No, Lake Wauburg. You know where it is?"

"South of the motel, across Paynes Prairie, right?" she said.

"Right." I confirmed.

Continuing our, twisting, passing, backward walking conversation, we made plans to meet at Lake Wauburg on Saturday morning—for a *picnic*. Finally, the line straightened to the long registration table where UF staff took sweat crumpled forms and input them into the computer. Unsettling cries of "You've got to be kidding me!" echoed off the cavernous walls. We all knew that meant a class had closed right before that student handed them their form. Kristina made it through no problem. But there wasn't nearly as many engineering students signing up for thermodynamics as there were business undergrads vying for economics.

Approaching the registration table, my pulse quickened with the passing of each student ahead of me. I saw

Kristina, waiting to the side, straining to see if I made it through. I hoped to walk her back to her car—to embrace her, to kiss her.

Handing my class registration form to the lady at the table, I continued looking at Kristina. I could hardly wait to get outside with her.

"Econ 201, M-W-F at 10 a.m. is closed. You'll have to pick another class. Please move to the back of the line," jolted me from fantasyland.

"What? No, it was open!"

"I'm sorry, it's closed. Please move," she said with an exasperated tone. Registration wasn't a fun experience for anyone, staff included.

I wanted to ring the neck of the a-hole who took the last space in *my* class. I looked over to Kristina waiting for me at the entrance. Shaking my head, no, she knew what had happened. "See you Saturday," I mouthed silently over the throng of students.

She nodded. "I've got to go," she mouthed back with an empathetic smile.

# 61

## HELGI

It was the week before my planned rendezvous with Kristina. Grandma was manning the front desk when I walked into the office. Both Mom and Dad were outside speaking with two elderly women. A large tow truck was maneuvering a U-Haul truck into a parking space. Guests at the pool pointed at the side of the U-Haul. The side I couldn't see.

"Hey, what's happening, Grandma?"

"An accident. Leena asked me to take over while she and Sven went out to help those ladies," she said, pressing her upper dentures into the Polygrip.

"Need any help here?"

"No, I've got this covered. Pretty slow today."

"Cool, I'm going out to see what's shaking'."

There was an instinct within our family to rally the troops, so to speak, any time we had some sort of commotion at the motel. More than simple curiosity, it was a defensive move. Like a herd gathering in a circle for protection from a threat, it was part of the lifestyle.

Drawing close to the folks, I could tell the ladies were upset. Mom held one of the women, who cried. The other lady spoke to Dad. Walking around the U-Haul, I saw a huge gaping hole at the top on the passenger side. The truck was jam-packed with moving boxes, some torn open exposing clothing and personal items. These people's lives were stripped bared for all to see. I veered off to the room Hester was cleaning to get the scoop.

"Hey, Hester."

"Morning, baby."

"Know what's up with those two ladies?"

"Well, you knows I minds my own business, but Is overheard something bout an accident. Seems the two ladies are sisters. The one was hepin' her sister an' her husband move to Ocala from up north. They be cutting through Gainesville to get off the highway. Parrently, the Mr., who be drivin' the truck, had a stroke and ran plum into the viaduct on 13$^{th}$. The ambulance took him to Shands.

"That sucks."

"I know. It be sad for them ladies. Specially the wife."

They had the movin' van towed here. Needed someplace cheap to stay. Cops toldem' bout the Florida Motel. Ms. Leena told me to get a double ready right fast."

"Figures, they're here all the time." I turned to leave. "Thanks Hester. I knew you'd have the scoop."

"Always count your blessins' baby," she said. "Speakin' of blessins', I hears that girl, Ms. Kristina, came by to see you."

I twisted around to face Hester again. "How'd you… never mind. What did Mom tell you?" I asked, expecting to hear about gold-diggers or sluts.

Ms. Leena says she was a nice girl. Pretty little thing with good manners. Told me she could tell she really likes you n' you her."

"Mom said nice things about Kristina?"

"That an' bout the pool," she said with a grin.

I blushed. "Well, what can I say? You know I *really* like her."

"What ol' Hester tell you bout women?"

"Yeah, yeah, you were right…as usual. She came all the way down from the north side of town to see me."

"Did you tells' her how you feels bout her?" she asked like a prosecutor.

Well, I think it was obvious how we felt about each in the pool," I said with a bit of pride.

"Feeling her up isn't the same as tellin', baby."

"Did Mom say anything else?"

"You knows us moms. We have super eyes and we knows what be happinin' under blankets…or water." She smirked while flying clean linens over one of the double beds. "You probly shouldn't be climin' up the slide when Ms. Kristina be visitin'."

Cringing, I put my hands over my face. "Crap, Mom saw that?"

"Oh yeah, baby, she saw every*thing*." Hester was having too much fun with this.

"C'mon, give me a break," I pleaded.

"You goin' to tell that girl how you feel or do Hester need to slap you upside the head?"

"Okay, okay, I'll tell her. I mean it this time."

"When? When you be tellin' her? Better be real soon. You hears me, baby?"

"This Saturday. We have a date. Going on a picnic at Lake Wauburg.

"Well, that sounds nice. You behave now—hear?" she smiled with approval.

I headed back to the office. Mom pulled out of the parking lot with the two ladies in our car and Dad began tying blue tarp over the gash in the U-Haul.

"Hey Grandma, where's Mom going?"

"She's taking those ladies over to Shands. They're pretty upset. Leena offered to drive and keep them company. She asked us to hold down the fort."

"Of course. Why don't you take a little break? I'll watch the desk."

Dad had given them a discounted rate, including the weekend which was a home game for the Gators. My folks were simply doing the right thing for people in trouble. The Florida Motel would become a sanctuary for these ladies—a place to help them through the trauma of the accident and the uncertainty of the husband's stroke. A temporary home where they could take time to sort things out. It was another one of those moments that stopped me in my tracks—made me think and reevaluate the motel life. I was proud of my parents.

# 62

# KRISTINA

Kristina felt a twinge of nervous excitement as she turned the key of the mustang. It was early on a Saturday morning. Telling her parents she needed a full day at the library to study for finals, was the first time she'd ever lied to them in her life. Well, maybe the second if you count the omission of the Halloween Ball when she talked to her dad about Helgi. She didn't want anything or anyone getting in the way of their *picnic*. She thought something special might happen today.

As she drove past the Florida Motel on her way to Lake Wauburg, thoughts of that day in the pool with Helgi simmered deep inside. Her heart began racing as she crossed Paynes Prairie. The morning fog forcing her to slow down only intensified the anticipation of being alone with him. Away from the watchful eyes of his mother and the interruptions of the motel. Driven by expectations of what might happen, intense sensations welled to the surface reaching every nerve in her body.

Turning into the lake's dirt parking area, she spotted Helgi standing next to his car.

*God, I want him.*

# 63

## HELGI

I had paced back and forth in the dirt parking area for twenty minutes, waiting to spend the day with Kristina far from the prying eyes of my mother and the distractions of the motel. The feelings and urges were strong between us, but this was a big step. I worried she might not come. My heart jumped into high gear when I saw the burgundy Mustang turn into the entrance off *the road*. Trying to be cool, I waved from folded arms as she parked next to me, but my giddy, ear-to-ear smile gave me away. I admired Kristina's lovely shape as she got out of her car. She was sexy in the tight, blue satin shorts she wore.

"Hey."

"Hey."

Kristina stopped in front of me and tipped her head—our lips inches away. We kissed.

Stepping back, she lifted her arm. "I brought a picnic basket.

"That's nice." I smiled. Food was the last thing on my mind.

We grabbed the basket and some towels and headed down to the lake. The sun had burned off the morning fog and now reflected warmly off the water.

"Canoe or rowboat? I asked.

"Canoe. I want to help paddle."

"No complaints from me."

Making our way down to the shoreline, we saw several groups of students already set up along the beach. Some played Frisbee in the water or were at the sand volleyball court getting a game together. Others sunbathed. A lifeguard perched atop one of those oversized chairs kept watch over the beachfront. Owned by UF, Lake Wauburg was primarily used for student recreation. They had canoes, row boats and sailboats that students could check out at no cost. The swimming area had a floating platform for jumping into the lake and sunbathing.

All the canoes were lined up along the shore, half out of the water. Made of aluminum, they were cheap, easy to maintain and practically indestructible. But they would get blistering hot under the Florida sun. We checked one out, grabbed two paddles and the required life jackets that no one ever wore. I tossed the jackets in the bottom as Kristina gingerly stepped in and took the seat out front.

"Here's your paddle." I handed it to her, laid the other one next to my seat, and placed the picnic basket in the middle.

As I shoved the canoe, the sandy shore let go of its

grip, and we gently floated into the water. We paddled in sync to the far side of the lake.

"Do you think we'll see gators?" she asked in a small-talk way. As a bona fide local, she knew that in Florida where there's water there are gators.

"Yes, but not as many as Lake Alice."

"Why's that?"

"No one feeds them here, so they don't come over when they see us. We only need to stay away from their nests. They will attack if you threaten their eggs."

"Well, let's not do that," she said paddling.

The lake was as smooth as a freshly-made Hester bed. We made it to the other side in no time. Nearing the far shore, we pulled in the paddles and laid them over the seats. Silently drifting, we took in the sights for a few minutes. The one I enjoyed the most was Kristina's slender back leading down to two dimples right above her cute rear end.

She pointed at a log. "Look at those beautiful birds. What are they?"

"Dimples," I murmured.

"Dimples?"

"Uh…ducks," I stammered, getting a fix on the fowl. "Wood ducks. The one with the head full of colored feathers is the male."

"Showoffs. Don't the alligators eat them?" she asked.

"No, they're too fast, and they nest up in the trees." We inched along the shoreline. The serene calm coaxed my real emotions to the surface. I knew why I was in a canoe on the far side of Lake Wauburg on a Saturday morning.

*Was she there for the same reason?*

## 64

## KRISTINA/HELGI

Kristina sensed he was looking at her backside. She knew why she was there. For all her type-A-engineer logical thinking, physical passion and sexual desire overwhelmed her. Like the day at the pool, something had taken over her heart, mind and body. Every nerve in her body exploded with each touch of his hands. For the first time in her life, she felt out of control…and loved it!

*Is he thinking the same thing? Is this being horny? I think I'm horny. "Horny" what a funny word.*

---

A slight breeze stirred, cooling our skin. Kristina's hair drifted over her face as she turned to face me. Leaning toward each other, our lips came together. The canoe jostled. We had to be careful, or we would capsize. To lower our center of gravity, we slid off our seats, kneeling close on the canoe's floor, heightening our passions. With her eyes locked into mine, she reached behind her back. Kristina unhooked her bikini top, let it slip off her shoulders, and fall away. She blushed as she presented herself to me.

---

T*his is for you—only you, my dear Helgi.* No one had ever seen her naked body. *I'm so scared. Oh God, his hands are touching my…*

---

B*eautiful breasts* I kissed her and ran my hands down the sides of her body and around her waist. I moved my hands between us, the tips of my fingers brushing her erect nipples. Kristina inhaled with a low moan and arched her back. My lips moved along her neck as I caressed her soft, firm breasts.

"Umm, oh…ouch," she said.

"What's wrong?" *…am I pinching her or something?*

"The canoe rivets are digging into my knees."

"Get the towels."

She reached over her head to grab them while I planted a kiss where my hand had been. Nothing would distract me from my duties. Kristina sighed before we hastily broke away from each other to spread the towels on the bottom of the canoe.

"Grab the life preservers too. We can use them as pillows," I said between shallow breaths.

We slid to the bottom and lay on the bed of towels. Kissing led to writhing in a tangle of arms and legs. About to do what Hester said I shouldn't, my hands explored every part of her gorgeous body. My tongue throbbed deep inside her mouth. Kristina responded in kind, sending lightning bolts through my body.

---

Kristina moaned. She lost all inhibitions as Helgi's fingers brushed over her breasts and then gently held them in his hands. Every inch of her was in a state of intense sexual arousal. Her instincts took over as she slid her palms over his torso and under his shorts.

*OMG, I'm touching his…! So that's what it looks like. Wait…it goes where?*

# 65

# HELGI

Navigating in uncharted waters without a compass, nothing in our Sex-Ed classes in middle school had prepared us for the tempest of sensations reeling through every molecule of our being. We were rising on the crest of a sexual storm, and there would be no turning back.

Excited and terrified, the little voice in my head still got my attention. It told me this wasn't how it was meant to be with her. Kristina was different, special. Not some girl, but *the* girl.

"Oh…mmm, Helgi, Helgi."

"Kristina, are you? Do you want to…?"

"Yes, yes. Did you bring…?"

"Yes." I reached for the foil packet buried in my shorts. The canoe rocked from side to side as we tossed off the rest our clothes.

"… mmm…ooh…aah…," echoed from the love boat. The narrow sides of the canoe acted like a speaker, amplifying our moans all over the lake.

"Careful," I cautioned as Kristina maneuvered to the middle. I straddled over her to center our weight. We didn't want our fondling to cause us to flounder. The rocking settled. Peering into Kristina eyes, I shook with excitement and fumbled with the condom. Finally, successful with protection installation, I rose over her as she spread like a butterfly opening its wings for the very first time. I could hardly believe I was about to lose my virginity with her. Our hearts pounded. Our senses screamed. We looked into each other's eyes.

"Kristina."

"Helgi."

"Nice ass!"

"*What*? Who said that?" Kristina's eyes locked on mine.

"What?" I said, continuing to lower myself to her body.

"Woot, woot…go for it dude! Jump all over that!" ricocheted off the canoe.

"Helgi!" Kristina panicked.

"I didn't say any…oh shit!" Horror replaced ecstasy.

We froze in place like a pair of stunned rabbits caught in the act. From bent knees, I turned toward the mysterious voices and peered over the side of the canoe. There before my eyes was a rowdy group of students looking down at us from the swim deck.

"What is it, Helgi?"

"The breeze pushed us back across the lake. We're right in front of the beach."

My beautiful butterfly snapped shut her wings. "Oh my God!" she said. Pulling herself into a ball, Kristina tucked and rolled to the opposite side of the canoe, hitting me in the nuts with her knee. My eyes slid to the back of my head as the pain of being kneed radiated through me. The canoe tipped hard to the side, causing both paddles to fall out. Then it rolled hard toward the beach. We were fully exposed. A raucous roar of approval erupted from our new fan club. Disheveled and red faced, Kristina yanked the up the towels and attempted to cover herself. I flipped over to the side to dive out of sight. Unfortunately, my still erect dick slammed right into the searing hot, aluminum hull.

"Ouch! I screeched while pulling myself into a fetal position.

"What do we do, Helgi?" Kristina pleaded. "The paddles are floating away."

"Use your hands," I told her, groaning in pain. Flopping an arm over the side, I frantically thrashed at the water.

"Helgi, what about the gators?"

"Gators! Don't worry about the damn gators. They're all on the other side of the lake. They don't like the beach. Just paddle!" I ordered like a captain going down with his ship.

"Do it. Do it. Do it," rang out from overhead.

Kristina inched herself up the side of the canoe enough for her arm to reach over to the water. She let it hover for a moment before plunging it in the lake and began paddling with all her might. Slowly, the we began moving away from the beach.

"I don't think they can see us anymore," I said.

"Check to make sure," she whispered as if that would help her hide.

I poked my head up and looked back toward the

beach. We were far enough away. "All clear," I said, while lurching backward to the center.

We lay there, silent, side by side and buck naked as the canoe drifted over the surface of the lake. Kristina's towel, askew over her body, looked like a messed-up toga.

Was this one of those bad endings I so desperately wanted to avoid? Would this be the thing that destroys our relationship? Hester warned me not to do this. I thought I'd really screwed things up, but then Kristina started to giggle. Then I giggled. The giggling led to laughter, and I had my answer. She was cool with it, and with me.

"Watcha going to do with that?" she pointed at the condom precariously hanging on to my…um…deflated "passion."

"Toss it in the lake," I answered. Then I removed it and flipped it overboard.

"But a gator might eat it," she exclaimed.

"Now you're worried *for* the gators. Really?"

"Hey, I have an idea for the next time," she said.

*Next time.* I smiled. "What's that?"

"Use the anchor."

She wanted to see me again. There couldn't have been a better moment to tell her how I felt.

*Here we go, Hester.*

"Kristina?"

"Yes, Helgi?"

"I love you."

"I love you too, Helgi. I knew it the day we met."

We held hands and stared up at the blue sky. Billowy white clouds that looked like Hester-approved, properly-puffed pillows, floated over the two lovebirds cradled in the bottom in a canoe. Then we both broke into laughter once again, this time at the thought of an alligator cruising around Lake Wauburg with a rubber stuck on its snout.

# 66

# HELGI

I was at the front desk when my new friend from number nine entered the office.

“Morning,” I said.

“Hey man, how’s your dad doing?” he asked.

“He’s all healed up. Hundred percent back to normal.”

“That’s good news. I came in to settle my bill. Time for me to hit the road.” He pulled out a roll of cash held tight by a rubber band.

I gave him the total, collected the payment and handed him a receipt.

“Hey, I can’t thank you enough for helping us that night,” I said.

“It was nothing. Glad to be of service again.”

“Where you off to?”

“Wherever the road takes me, as long as my feet hold up,” Number Nine replied with a warm smile breaking through the sun leathered skin of his crinkled face. His eyes spoke of much evil and pain that had passed through them, but a glint of hope still could be seen deep inside. "Listen kid, you've got a good thing going here. You're going places. Become somebody. When you get there, don't forget where you came from."

"I know. I won't. Come back anytime," I said.

Number Nine hefted his knapsack, stuffed with all his worldly possessions, up over his shoulder, turned and walked out the office door. I was sorry for the things I had said and thought about him. He went from a stoner I shamelessly called Fogman, to discarded Vietnam Vet who instinctively protected our family to philosopher. People who would see him on the road would call him a bum. To me, he would always be a hero. It was the last time we saw Number Nine.

Content, I looked out over the parking lot and around the motel. A family unloaded their station wagon. The band girls sunbathed by the pool. Hester waltzed through the rooms to the tune of Amazing Grace while Dad fixed the door lock on number fifteen. Professor Lockwood must have worn it out during "office hours." From inside the living quarters, I heard Mom and Grandma jabbering about something or nothing, in the kitchen. A great blue heron flew over on its way to the prairie. The shadow from its huge wings floated over our big neon sign as if to say "thank you" for guiding him home. I too had come home. Home to the Florida Motel.

Reflecting on the past couple of months, a strange thought stuck me. I didn't feel jealous of the students who lived on campus. I wouldn't trade places with any frat boy or dorm rat. I realized the motel wasn't holding me prisoner. Rather, it had helped me grow up. Taught me how to run a business and more importantly what matters in life. It provided a new friend and mentor in the most unlikely person in the world—Hester the maid. But most of all, when I thought I had lost my soul mate forever, this crazy place brought her back to me.

With heartfelt joy, I opened my calculus text and turned to Kristina, "Ready, Tutor?"

"Absolutely, Pool Boy. I owe you for that 'A' I got in English Comp."

# ABOUT THE AUTHOR

Jay Gilbert was born and raised on a farm in Duluth, MN. One of five boys, his father kept them out of trouble (mostly) with a host of daily chores caring for horses, cows, chickens, and ducks. If they weren't feeding the animals at the front end, they were shoveling what came out of the back end. His family owned and operated small businesses ranging from a ship chandlery, vacuum shop, electronics store, and a motel.

Their businesses took them from Minnesota to Illinois, and finally to Florida.

Between farm life and family business, Jay has collected an eclectic inventory of experiences that form the basis for his stories. Jay lives and writes by the lessons his parent taught him.

---

Dad always said, "Life is not a dress rehearsal. There are no do-overs."

Mom taught us how to say "Please" and Thank you," and mean it.

---

Thank you for reading **The Florida Motel**.

If you enjoyed Helgi's story, kindly leave a review on Amazon and/or wherever you purchased the book. He needs all the encouragement he can get.

---

Connect with me at gilbertjay58@gmail.com or visit wwwseaquillwriters.com and find me under Featured Authors.

ALSO BY JAY GILBERT

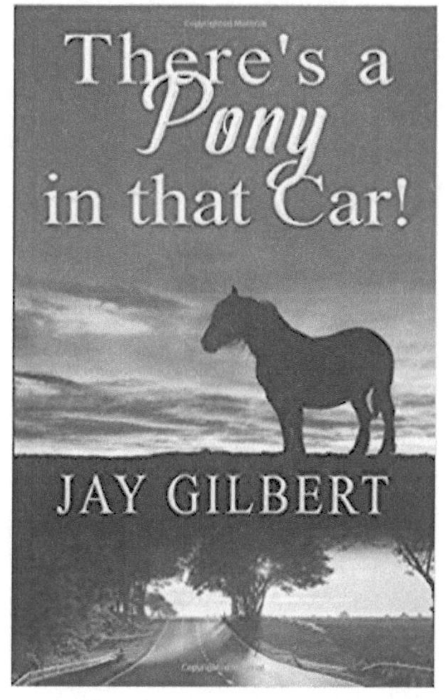


**There's A Pony in That Car!**

www.ingramcontent.com/pod-product-compliance
Lightning Source LLC
Chambersburg PA
CBHW020551310726
48979CB00008B/1176/J

* 9 7 8 1 9 5 0 9 4 0 1 3 4 *